HORSES OF

HALF MOON
RANCH

JETHRO JUNIOR

D1079826

HORSES OF
Half Moon
RANCH

JETHRO JUNIOR

JENNY OLDFIELD

Illustrated by
Paul Hunt

Hodder
Children's
Books

a division of Hodder Headline

Special thanks to the children of Carrington Junior School,
Flackwell Heath.

With thanks also to Bob, Karen and Katie Foster, and to the staff
and guests at Lost Valley Ranch, Deckers, Colorado

Typeset by Avon Dataset Ltd, Bidford-on-Avon, Warks

Printed and bound in Great Britain by
The Guernsey Press Co. Ltd, Channel Isles

Hodder Children's Books
a division of Hodder Headline Ltd
338 Euston Road
London NW1 3BH

1

'The heat is on!' Charlie Miller announced over the loudspeaker. 'The two teams are neck and neck as we reach the last, vital stage of the competition!'

Kirstie Scott grinned at her friend, Lisa Goodman. There was a lot to grin about: the hot sun, the ice-capped mountains in the distance, the hurly-burly of the Half-Moon Ranch Horse Olympics.

'That Charlie!' Lisa laughed. She sat on the fence rail of the arena, nodding towards the

1

young, enthusiastic wrangler as he announced the final event of the afternoon. 'He sure has come out of his shell lately!'

Kirstie raised her eyebrows but said nothing. Maybe Lisa had a crush on Charlie.

'First to go is staff member Ben Marsh on the big sorrel, Silver Flash. Way to go, Ben!' Charlie's voice whipped up excitement among the watching guests, staff and neighbouring ranchers. The Fun Olympics had attracted a crowd of around one hundred and fifty to the remote outfit at the end of Five Mile Creek Trail.

Kirstie clapped and cheered along with the rest as head wrangler Ben loped Silver Flash around the arena. The sorrel's coat glistened a rich nut-brown in the bright sunlight, the white blaze down her face making her look proud and beautiful. 'She's got a good chance of coming out the winner, I reckon,' Kirsty murmured appreciatively.

As if to prove her point, Ben took Silver Flash over the first log without a problem. In fact, they cleared the jump with a couple of feet to spare.

'Hmm.' Lisa jutted out her chin, swinging her leg over the rail and jumping to the ground. She was on her way to the corral to mount her own horse in the competition. 'Don't be too sure,' she warned Kirstie. 'Just you wait until Hollywood Princess gets a chance to show what she can do!'

Still grinning, Kirstie ran alongside Lisa. 'Hey, this is supposed to be a Fun Olympics, remember! Don't go breaking your neck over those bigger logs!'

Lisa nipped between a group of spectators including her grandfather, Lennie Goodman, the vet, Glen Woodford, and the Forest Ranger, Smiley Gilpin. Smiley gave her a slap on the back and wished her good luck as he saw her jump into Hollywood's saddle. 'Way to go, Lisa!' he called.

Meanwhile, the crowd cheered another success for Ben and Silver Flash in the arena. Clear so far, and with only four more jumps to go.

Then, as the sorrel attempted a three-foot pole resting on a pair of upturned oil barrels, Kirstie heard a gasp and a sigh.

Glancing across, she saw that the fence was down. Silver Flash spooked at the sound of the rolling pole, broke her stride and careered off to the left, flinging his rider sideways. Ben kept his seat, but the horse's concentration was ruined.

They ended up bringing down the next fence, which put them in third position at the end of the round.

'Next to ride is . . .' The loudspeaker system crackled as Charlie checked his list '. . . Lisa Goodman on Hollywood Princess.'

Kirstie saw the beautiful albino horse's ears prick up at the sound of her name. She pranced a couple of steps towards the arena, arched her neck and got ready to go.

'Good luck!' Opening the gate to let them through, Kirstie gave Lisa a thumbs up signal. Then she stood on the fence to watch.

Jeez, was Hollywood a magnificent creature! Pure white, Arab-looking with that dished nose and big, dark eyes. She was gorgeous. And didn't she just know it! The way she lifted those feet and eased into a trot showed she had attitude. And that was Attitude with a capital 'A'.

Over the first easy log and coasting, Lisa swung Hollywood towards the second. The horse sailed over the jump with disdain. The spectators cheered the glamorous pair and got right behind them as they approached the oil-drum fence.

'Go-go-go, Lisa!' Charlie called down the microphone.

Kirstie grinned to herself.

'What's with you?' her brother Matt asked as, still smiling, she jumped down and went to mount her own horse in the competition. She was enjoying herself so much thinking about Charlie and Lisa that she'd almost bumped into him. Now he caught hold of her white stetson as it tipped from her head and jammed it back in place on top of her long, fair hair.

'Nothing. A girl can grin if she likes!' Kirstie replied. 'Let go, Matt; I need to find my horse.'

'You're planning something, I can tell,' he said suspiciously.

'Only to do my best to help win the competition,' she assured him. She was in the Eagle's Peak team with Ben and four other riders. Lisa was part of the Hummingbird Rock team, along with ranch owner Sandy Scott. After the barrel racing and the reining sections, the score between the two sides was pretty even, and as Charlie had said a while ago, the heat was definitely on.

In more ways than one. This was high summer.

Even at a height of 8,000 feet, the temperature was scorching. Clear blue skies and a sheltered valley had baked the pale yellow earth hard and reduced the water flow in Five Mile Creek to half its winter volume. And the ranch sat in the base of this natural oven; a cluster of red roofs shaded by dark, tall pine trees but still sweltering in the heat.

'I put your horse in a stall inside the barn to stay cool,' Matt told Kirstie, leading the way through the wide doors. 'I guess you'd prefer to be riding Lucky, huh?'

Lucky was Kirstie's very own palomino. And sure, there was no horse like him for smart thinking and loyalty. But he was out of action with a hock sprain and Glen Woodford had ordered pasture rest for him up at Aspen Valley. Lucky would be up there for the rest of the summer, living a lazy life, while Kirstie helped Ben break in a new Connemara-cross.

And this was the horse Matt had saddled for her to ride in the jumping competition. Here he was, tethered inside the dark, cool barn, listening to the crowd cheer Lisa and Hollywood to a clear round.

'No penalty points!' Charlie announced. 'In a super-fast time of three minutes, twenty seconds. Beat that, Eagle's Peak team!'

'Hey, Jethro, you hear that?' Kirstie went up to the dark bay gelding and stroked his soft muzzle. She breathed a few words into his ear. 'Hollywood just went clear, so now it's down to us!'

'Just quit the horse-whispering stuff and get up in that saddle!' Matt told her to get a move on. 'Charlie's waiting to announce you.'

So she swung up on to the little horse's broad back and made for the dazzling square of daylight and the corral beyond.

'Last to ride is ranch favourite, Kirstie Scott, on newcomer, Jethro Junior!' Charlie paved the way for their entrance into the arena.

There was a buzz in the crowd, a keen sense that Kirstie's round could make the difference between winning and losing for her team. Then everything fell quiet as Jethro trotted into view.

Kirstie felt the silent attention focus in on her and her horse. So, Jethro wasn't drop-dead gorgeous, like Hollywood Princess. He didn't even look especially athletic, like Silver Flash. Maybe the spectators were a little disappointed

7

by the look of him. Dark bay, almost black, he was short of stature. In fact, he didn't quite make fourteen hands. But the thing about Jethro was that he was willing.

More than willing. Kirstie had found this out by riding the trails around the ranch with him. He'd go all day and never tire, and he'd still be up for more when the likes of Hollywood were sighing and groaning and saying, *Give me my hay and water, brush me down and let me sleep!*

Jethro's sturdiness came from his part-Irish breeding, and Kirstie liked to imagine his ancestors climbing the rocky roads and roaming the wild, high hills of the west coast of Ireland. Connemaras were a plucky breed who never let you down, and this combined with the endurance qualities of a good quarter-horse made Jethro Junior a joy to ride.

But as she trotted him around the arena, even Kirstie had to admit she didn't know how well the small gelding would do over these high jumps.

Short legs probably equals limited jumping ability, she told herself as they got ready to take the first low log. She waited for the bell to signal the start of their round, aware that she'd never really had the chance to test out Jethro's skill.

Two weeks on the ranch wasn't long to get to know him properly. Old Hadley Crane, the ex-head wrangler at Half-Moon Ranch, had found Jethro in San Luis sale barn. The old man's expert eye for a horse had picked out the Connemara-cross from more spectacular-looking candidates.

'Born and bred in New Mexico,' he'd told Kirstie, who'd gone along to the sale with him. 'Which accounts for him being shorter in the leg and stockier than the plains horses from further north. Four years old, coming off a ranch south of Albuqerque. Good running on him. Willing attitude. I'd say he'd do us just fine!'

'So let's prove Hadley right!' Kirstie murmured under her breath as they headed for the start of the course. Charlie sat at his table, ready to press the bell. Hadley stood behind him, catching Kirstie's eye and giving her a brief nod of encouragement.

The bell sounded, the clock began to tick.

'Go, Jethro!' Kirstie whispered.

The little horse shot forward like a coiled spring. He belted towards the log at a flat-out gallop, took it without breaking his stride, then swept around the outside of the arena in response to Kirstie's next reining command. He took a brushwood fence without even noticing it, finding a perfect rhythm and approaching the obstacle with total boldness.

'Yeah!' the crowd yelled. This little horse might not look much, but he sure could jump!

'Way to go, Kirstie!'

Kirstie picked out Lisa's high-pitched yell from the rest. They might be on opposing teams, but friendship won out in the end.

Anyway, this was for fun!

But Jethro didn't think so as he hurtled through the course. He took the barrels-and-pole at breakneck speed, soared over it then turned on the spot, ready for the last run of barriers.

Another brushwood; tall and wide. The bay flew over it, cleared the far side by a mile.

Then a pole resting on the top of two upright barrels at a height of about four feet. Kirstie felt Jethro gather himself and judge the challenge. She urged him on. And the little guy flew at this one too; so fast that her hat blew off and dangled down her back, held in place by the thin leather chinstrap. And her fair hair flew free in the rush of wind caused by Jethro's heroic leap.

One more fence: a solid tree trunk resting on the ground, its bark scaling off and leaving paler patches, some lopped off branches still looking dangerously jagged and sharp.

'Go, Jethro! Go, Kirstie!' they yelled.

Jethro threw himself at the obstacle, leaned back into his haunches, took off and cleared it with ease.

Kirstie felt him land safely. She heard Charlie announce their clear round and a time of three minutes five seconds. She let go of the reins and raised both arms in the air. Victory for the Eagle's Peak team! A major triumph for gutsy little Jethro Junior!

'Hot, hot, hot!' Lisa sighed.

The Fun Olympics were over. It was early evening and the ranch was still crowded with guests and neighbours. So she and Kirstie had taken off for a quiet bend in Five Mile Creek.

'Is that the weather we're talking about here?' Kirstie quizzed. She was wearing her bathing-suit and a pair of denim shorts, really looking forward to a dip in the cool clear water of the creek. So

11

she quickly dumped her towel on the grassy bank and stepped out of her shorts.

'Yeah!' Lisa gave her a sideways look. 'What else?'

'I thought maybe when you said "hot", you were meaning Charlie.'

'Kirstie Scott, how could you!' Lisa squealed. 'Charlie works here. I never even thought about him in that way!'

'No?'

'No way! Just because I pass a remark about him earlier doesn't mean I find him attractive or anything.'

'Sure.' Kirstie shrugged, turned her back and dipped one toe in the creek to test out the water. She was balancing on one leg and should've known better than to tease Lisa from that position.

Whoosh! Lisa came down the bank and gave Kirstie's shoulders a firm push from behind. One second Kirstie was hovering on the bank, the next she hit the water face-down. She went under, then came up gasping and flailing her arms in all directions. 'You louse!' she cried. 'This creek is c-co-cold!'

Lisa jumped in beside her, newly confident in

her swimming skills. Kirsty had made sure she'd taught her after a scary near-drowning experience on the ranch. Now Lisa surfaced with her mass of dark auburn curls plastered to her head, her freckled face bobbing close to Kirstie's. 'So anyways, how about you and Ben?'

'Ben . . . ? Ben's ancient!' Kirstie protested. A lovely, quiet, shy guy, but truly ancient. He was 27.

'So's Charlie,' Lisa pointed out.

'He's twenty, the same age as Matt.' Kirstie loved the cool feel of the water against her limbs as she turned on to her back and flapped around idly in the gently swirling current.

'Yeah, right. Exactly.' Lisa murmured, doing the same thing and gazing up at the early evening sky. 'Anyhow, don't you have enough romantic problems around here, without me falling for someone twice my age?'

'Charlie's not twice your age!'

Splash! Kick-splash-splash! from Lisa. End of conversation.

'How's your mom getting along with Brad lately?' Lisa moved the romance topic forward a step.

Brad Martin was new to the scene and causing

quite a stir at Half-Moon Ranch. Flashy in appearance, with his handmade cowboy boots and fringed shirts, he'd made it pretty plain from the start that Sandy Scott was his type of woman. Four or five years on from her divorce from Matt and Kirstie's dad, Sandy played along with Brad's flirting games, and Kirstie found she didn't mind too much. In fact, she liked Brad. He was kind and honest below the flashy surface, and the best reining rider in the whole state of Colorado.

It was Matt who objected to their mom's involvement with Brad. Hostile from the start, his suspicions had lessened over the months but had still not completely disappeared.

'It's the Cold War all over again between Matt and Brad,' Sandy had joked, trying to laugh it off after one of their small flare-ups.

Now, swimming in the creek after the excitement of the day's events, Kirstie found herself wishing that those complications could just dissolve away. 'Mom and Brad get along fine,' she told Lisa. 'And if Matt would stop being so pig-headed, the situation would be pretty much perfect.'

'Yeah, give me a simple relationship with a horse rather than a person any day!' Lisa sighed.

For some reason, the remark made them both burst out laughing. They began to shriek and flounder in the water, trying to touch the bottom, but finding they were out of their depth. The more they laughed and struggled, the more they gulped in water and began to choke.

'What? What's so funny?' Lisa croaked between coughs. She was swimming for the bank so that she could recover her breath.

'The fact that you prefer horses to humans, I guess!' Clumsily Kirstie followed Lisa. She hauled herself on to the bank and lay, belly-down, like a gasping fish out of water.

Lisa rolled away to a safe distance and lay on her back. 'That's the pot calling the kettle black if ever there was! I mean, here's a girl called Kirstie Scott who's totally nuts about every horse that ever breathed. And she has the sass to accuse me of preferring horses to people!'

'OK, OK!' Kirstie had to acknowledge that Lisa was right. She grabbed hold of her towel, spread it on the sloping grass and lay down to dry off. 'Fair point. But, did you ever meet a horse who *lied* to you, for example?'

'Pooh, cynic!' Lisa wanted to cling on to a little

bit of faith in the human species. 'But I agree with you in one way. If you treat a horse right, he gives you everything he's got.'

'Like Jethro Junior,' Kirstie pointed out. She felt the low sun on her back, breathed in the smell of the sun-scorched grass.

'Yeah, and Hollywood.' Lisa pondered for a few seconds. 'Hey, that horse sure didn't like to lose the jumping contest. When she realised she wasn't in line for first prize, why she dropped her head and stamped her foot like crazy!'

Kirstie laughed. 'Hollywood loves to be the centre of attention. And I guess her ego took a beating when little Jethro came out the winner.'

'He was really neat.' Lisa recalled the way the small horse had flown over the fences. 'Hey!' She sat up suddenly with the force of a new and definitely brilliant idea.

Kirstie groaned and turned her head to squint at her friend. 'Uh-oh!'

'No, really! I just had this excellent thought!' Lisa was gazing across the creek in the direction of Bear Hunt Trail. On the opposite bank, the hill rose steeply away from the water. It was littered with big granite boulders and lined with ponderosa pines, but there was a clear trail through to Smiley Gilpin's place at Red Eagle Lodge.

'Tell!' Kirstie couldn't bear the suspense. She had to know what Lisa had in mind.

'You know the section of Bear Hunt where the loggers worked recently, with that felled timber and stuff?'

'Yep.' Kirstie thought of a stretch of trail where the forestry people had thinned out the trees. Most of the timber had been taken away on giant trucks, but there were still signs of where the work had taken place, and a smell of resin in the air where it oozed like orange glue from the giant stubs of the felled trees. Suddenly she guessed what Lisa was thinking. She too sat up. 'Uh-oh!'

Lisa saw that Kirstie was up-to-speed. 'So, is it a good idea, or not?'

'Let me get this straight. You're talking about training Hollywood and Jethro to jump the Jaw-breaker?'

'Jaw-breaker' was the ranch's name for a felled tree which had been left behind by the loggers. It had fallen across the official trail and since the spring, Ben and the other trail leaders had had to form a new trail to one side because the log was too wide and high for the horses to jump. When Matt had tried it on Cadillac, even he had been forced to admit defeat. In fact, so far this summer, no one had succeeded in jumping the log.

'Yeah!' Lisa was up for the challenge. 'Me on Hollywood. You on Jethro.'

'But the Jaw-breaker!' Kirstie hesitated. It lay on a cluttered slope, the earth was dry and dusty – everything was against anyone being able to make that jump.

Except Hollywood and Jethro maybe.

Kirstie thought about it. After all, they'd proved themselves in the arena today. The American Albino and the Connemara-cross had been the star jumpers; no one else had come near.

And it would be great to train Jethro to meet the challenge. They could practise and work up to it slowly. There would be the incentive for him of staying one step ahead of showy Hollywood.

So Kirstie turned to Lisa with a similar glint in her eye. Something to work at for the rest of the summer. A good piece of healthy rivalry which would also improve their riding skills.

'Yeah, why not?' she said with a grin. 'The Jaw-breaker it is!'

2

'OK, Jethro, this is your chance!' Kirstie pointed the eager horse towards the first jump which she and Lisa had constructed on a stretch of flat scrubland recently cleared by the logging team. They'd set out a challenging course of brushwood jumps and wide logs to get both Jethro and Hollywood Princess in training for the ultimate test – the Jaw-breaker.

'Hold it!' Lisa cried, running into Kirstie's line of vision at the last moment in order to clear away a stray branch. 'No way do we want the horses' attention wandering from the job in hand,' she said as she dragged the twisted arm of ponderosa pine out of sight.

'OK!' Kirstie said again. She drew a deep breath, felt the strong muscles in Jethro's haunches bunch, ready to launch himself forward.

Giving his sides the smallest touch with her heels, she set him loping at the first jump.

Soft hands and soft eyes. She kept in mind the Half-Moon Ranch basic rule for riding. It was the Horse Bible according to both Hadley Crane and Brad Martin, picked up from a guy called Ray Hunt who was famous the world over for his skill in working with horses.

Soft hands meant 'Don't overcorrect. Don't jerk at the reins because the gentlest pressure will do.' Soft eyes meant keeping alert to where the horse was putting his feet, allowing him to pick his own way over the ground you were asking him to cover. You went with him, kept a perfect balance, used your voice and legs to persuade him to do your thing when needed.

It was difficult stuff, but Brad had told Kirstie that she had a gift for it. 'You do it without having to think,' he'd pointed out. 'Like you're part of the horse and he's part of you.'

And that was how she felt, with Jethro galloping towards the log, her fair hair and his black mane both flying in the wind, linking their bodies in a harmonious whole.

His hooves thumped into the soft earth; she leaned forward against the saddle horn to avoid an overhanging branch. So her weight was already out of the saddle, where it should be to take the jump, when finally Jethro soared into the air with a glorious leap that took him well clear and allowed him to thunder on over the flat ground.

'Yee-hah!' Lisa cried from her position as a spectator. She yelled more encouragement as Kirstie and Jethro flew over the home-made course.

'Good boy!' Kirstie told him as he landed safely over the final log. She leaned forward to stroke his strong neck, noticed that he was breathing hard, so eased him gently into a trot and then a walk as she made a U-turn to go and rejoin Lisa.

'Neat!' Lisa smiled at her, then went quickly to untether Hollywood from a nearby tree. It was their turn.

'C'mon, girl, let's show 'em!' Hopping into the

saddle, Lisa made for the start of the course.

With the Albino's coat shining pure white under the sun, and with her proud, high-stepping walk, Kirstie realised that she and Jethro had a tough challenge if they wanted to be the first to jump the giant log, the dreaded Jaw-breaker itself.

'See that, Jethro?' she murmured, as Lisa aimed Hollywood at the first practice log. The glamour-horse lengthened her stride and took it disdainfully. 'That's beautiful, classy jumping out there!'

Standing in the shade, listening and watching, the little bay tossed his head. His bit and bridle seemed to jangle in defiance at the idea that drop-dead-gorgeous Hollywood could come anywhere near a Connemara-cross in the jumping stakes.

He stamped his front foot as if to say, *What's class and looks got to do with it?*

Kirstie translated his impatient footwork, then replied. 'Nope, don't be fooled,' she argued. 'Hollywood has a lot more than great looks going for her. She's got true grit beneath the flowing mane and tail, the dark eyelashes and the giant ego!'

To prove her point, Hollywood sailed over

every jump without even looking winded. When Lisa trotted her back to the start, she looked good and ready to go again.

'Yeah!' Kirstie gave her friend the high-five salute. 'Good job!'

'What d'you say we make the jumps a little higher?' Lisa asked breathlessly. Her grey-green eyes sparkled and her auburn hair had curled into an unruly halo in the warm breeze blowing off Bear Hunt Overlook.

'Do we have time before lunch?' Kirstie looked at her watch and saw that it was eleven-thirty. 'OK,' she decided, swinging out of the saddle and tying Jethro to a tree. 'Here's what we do. We build the new course, ride back to the ranch for a bite to eat, then come out with Jethro and Hollywood again towards evening.'

'Why wait so long?' An impatient Lisa had already set to dragging more brushwood out of a cleft in a granite boulder so she could start to build up the nearest fence.

'It's cooler when the sun goes down behind the Overlook,' Kirstie pointed out. 'We don't want to push Jethro and Hollywood too hard in the heat of the day.'

Lisa nodded. 'Right. I guess we have plenty of time.'

All the rest of the summer, as a matter of fact. No school, no distractions except the weekly influx of guests to Half-Moon Ranch, and the trail-riding, fun rodeos, evening square-dances and cook-outs that went with it. For a few moments, Kirstie broke off from watching Lisa drag the light branches across the ground and turned to take in the view.

Bear Hunt was one of her all-time favourite spots giving a three hundred and sixty degree view of the landmarks she'd grown to love on her five years at the ranch. She could see Eagle's Peak way in the distance at 13,000 feet. The mountain rose like a symmetrical cone, majestically huge and snow-capped, set against a deep blue sky.

Then, further along the horizon, there was Elk Rock and Shadow Rock, and beyond them, hazy glimpses of other mountains in the Meltwater Range.

Space! Kirstie thought. *And peace!*

'Hey, how come I'm doing all the work here?' Lisa's voice dragged her back to earth.

Grinning, Kirstie went to help her put more

wood on to the wide pile. 'Hot!' she sighed, as she stacked branches. She noticed the small blue butterflies dancing amongst the thorn bushes, heard the drone of insects and, further away, the *munch-crunch-grind* of Hollywood and Jethro's grazing jaws.

Ten minutes into the sweaty, scratchy job, both Lisa and Kirstie were glad of an unexpected interruption in the shape of a white Jeep trundling up Bear Hunt Trail.

'Hey, Smiley!' Lisa waved and called, recognising the Forest Ranger's logo on the hood of the four-wheel drive.

Smiley Gilpin leaned out and waved back. 'Hey, girls!'

'Who's that with you?' Kirstie was curious about a small figure standing in the back of the Jeep, hanging on to the roll-bars and enjoying the open-top experience of driving up a mountain on a hot summer's day.

'This is my grandson, Zachary.' Smiley drew to a halt about fifty yards from where the girls were working. 'He's on vacation with me up at Red Eagle Lodge while his mom and pop take a trip to Europe.'

'Neat!' Lisa smiled at the boy.

'Hey, Zach, how're you doing?' Kirstie watched Smiley climb out of his driving seat and lift the small boy over the side. Zachary looked to be about five years old; a lightly built kid with a pixie face and a spiky fringe of dark brown hair. When he grinned back at them, he showed them a bunch of pearly teeth.

'I'm doing just fine!' Zach replied.

'Is that a southern accent you have there, Zachary?' Kirstie thought she detected a lazy roll to his voice.

'Yes, ma'am. I live with my folks in Tampa, Florida.'

'Hey, so you get to go to Disney?'

'Yes, ma'am.'

'My name's Kirstie,' she smiled. 'And this is Lisa.'

'Nice to meet you,' said shy, polite little Zach, while his proud grandpa stood on the sidelines grinning from ear to ear.

'Zachary's helping me out with some important work,' Smiley explained, pulling a roll of leaflets from the back pocket of his jeans. 'Go ahead, son, explain to Kirstie and Lisa what we're doing with these.'

Zach pursed his mouth and thought it through. 'They're notices,' he began. 'They tell guys not to make fires in the forest because it's too dry.'

'OK – Fire Hazard notices.' Lisa nodded. 'Good job, Zach. We sure don't want folks tossing matches into the undergrowth or leaving camp-fires smouldering.'

'We nail them to the trees along the sides of the trails,' Zach went on earnestly. 'Grandpa says we have to put them where everyone can see, then they don't make a big mess of the forest.'

'I told him about the burn-out over on Tigawon Mountain just last summer.' Smiley recalled the raging fire that had destroyed acres of trees beyond Lone Elm Park. It had left the area a charred ruin of charcoal stumps and blackened earth; a kind of dark scar on the green beauty of the mountains. 'I said that this year we have to stop that kind of stuff from happening.'

'Do you want us to take some extra notices down to the ranch?' Kirstie suggested, thinking that they had noticeboards and doors they could pin the Fire Hazard warnings to. Then the ranch guests would be sure to take extra care too.

'Sure.' Smiley unrolled half a dozen and

handed them to Zachary to give to Kirstie. 'We already handed them out to the logging company and the guys who issue the gun licences for the hunting season.'

'Oh yeah.' Kirstie frowned. She'd forgotten that August was the month when the hunters came with their monster four-wheel drives and their rifles to persecute the poor, defenceless mule deer.

'Good boy, Zach.' A patient Smiley waited for his grandson to hand over the notices, then told him it was time to move on. 'We got a whole lot of trail to cover before we get to eat lunch.'

Zach scrambled up into the back of the Jeep unaided. 'Cold pizza!' he told Lisa and Kirstie. 'Grandpa brought us a sack lunch.'

'Yum!' Kirstie grinned up at him.

'And we got Hershey bars and marshmallows!'

Kirstie licked her lips. 'Stop – you're making me feel hungry!'

'You have a good day now,' Smiley said as he got in behind the wheel. He drove off up the trail with one happy grandson in the back of the Jeep, guarding a hammer, a roll of notices and a bag of nails as if his life depended on it.

'The Jaw-breaker, huh?' Brad Martin listened to Lisa's rapid description of the summer challenge that she and Kirstie had set themselves.

Brad and Charlie's group of Intermediate trail-riders had met the girls by Five Mile Creek at the end of an all-day ride. They'd stopped to talk and heard that Hollywood and Jethro were in training for a spot of serious jumping.

'You take it easy, you hear?' Charlie cut in with an anxious look in Lisa's direction. 'The Jaw-breaker earned it's name for a reason. It ain't easy to get over that sucker.'

Kirstie grinned to herself. She hummed a snatch of a romantic tune under her breath so that only Lisa could hear.

'Quit it, Kirstie!' Lisa blushed and flicked out with the ends of her reins.

'It ain't that hard.' Brad contradicted Charlie's warning, looking thoughtfully at the turn-off up Bear Hunt Trail where the girls were headed.

'Have you done it on Little Vixen?' Kirstie wanted to know.

'Yeah . . . well, no!' The brash cowboy had the grace to admit that he might be talking through the top of his high-crowned hat. 'We ain't actually attempted that baby, but I still say we could make it look easy.'

'Yeah, yeah!' Lisa knew a challenge when she heard one. 'So why not turn right around and show us?'

'Now?' Brad was taken aback. He felt the gaze of a dozen tired trail-riders fixed on his face. So he squared his shoulders. 'Sure!' he said. 'Charlie, you ride on home with these guys. I'll cut back with the girls and show them one classy piece of jumping!'

'You wish!' Kirstie grinned. Looking at Little Vixen, who was drooping slightly and who had hay and a good night's sleep firmly fixed in her head, she doubted that even Brad and his brilliant black-and-white paint could clear the giant log.

But she and Lisa enjoyed Brad's company as they took the trail and gained the shade of some tall pine trees. They got him to tell them about his youth on a cattle station in Montana, how it was so cut off he might not see another person for weeks or even months. 'It was a four hour ride to the nearest road,' he explained. 'That's a whole lot of solitude for a guy to experience.'

'No one to tell jokes to,' Lisa pointed out. 'No one to dress up in those fancy shirts and boots for!'

Teasing and joking, they soon made it to the section of Bear Hunt Trail where the loggers had worked and the strong smell of pine resin settled in their nostrils. The track gained in steepness and narrowed between tall pink rocks. Then it broadened out again to another recently deforested stretch.

'How far to the Jaw-breaker now?' Brad asked. He knew the trail less well than Kirstie and Lisa, and was looking out for landmarks that he could recognise.

'Across the Jeep road, past that stand of aspens.' Kirstie pointed out the area of shimmering green trees. 'You see where the land rises pretty steeply? That's the spot we're heading for.'

They approached quietly – no joking now, just concentrating on easing the horses up the incline, picking a route through the slender silver trunks of the aspens. Then, as they emerged from the trees, they were able to see the infamous log.

Resting horizontal across the narrow trail, its

roots had been ripped from the dry yellow earth and left exposed like long, twisted witches' fingers.

'Wow!' Brad drew Little Vixen up short. 'I forgot about the incline.'

From down below, the Jaw-breaker looked truly formidable. Probably four feet in diameter, it wasn't only a question of clearing that height, but of the horse gaining enough speed up the hill and being able to stretch wide enough to make it to the far side.

'Are you chickening out?' Lisa demanded.

Instead of replying, the reining champion clicked his tongue and urged Vixen slowly forward. They walked up to the obstacle, then Brad let the horse sniff around, wander this way and that to consider the question from all the angles.

'You gotta jump uphill,' Kirstie reminded Brad. 'The track's too steep to take the jump coming down.'

'I see that.' Brad reined his horse back down the hill, turning her neatly and getting her to take up a starting position some twenty yards below the giant log.

'You're sure Vixen can do it?' Kirstie asked quietly, her voice tense. Somehow, suddenly none of this seemed like a great idea. Inside her head, she pictured the clunk of Little Vixen's front hooves hitting the Jaw-breaker. She saw Brad thrown forward as the horse went down on her knees, imagined him lying spreadeagled on the earth with God knew how many bones broken. Or worse.

'One hundred per cent,' Brad assured her.

But the frown of concentration on his face didn't mirror the confidence of his reply. And

Kirstie realised that both Hollywood and Jethro had absorbed some of the new tension that was in the air, so that they started to sidestep and get jittery, looking as if the only thing they wanted was to head for home.

'Maybe you should come up to the practice area, put in some training first?' Lisa suggested.

Brad ignored her. He focused on the log, gave a single click of his tongue and waited for Vixen to start.

Vroom! The little paint set off like a tornado. Her speed came out of nowhere. One moment she was standing alert, ears pricked, eyes on the Jaw-breaker. The next she was rocketing off up the slope.

'Oh, I can't look!' Lisa squeezed her eyes shut and listened to the thud of Vixen's hooves.

Kirstie did the opposite; she stared hard. Every footfall echoed inside her head as Brad and Vixen reached their goal.

And then the horse was up, her front legs curled under her, her back legs kicking off with tremendous force.

And she was over, landing on the far side, stumbling slightly so that Brad had to adjust his position in the saddle to steady her. All four feet were safely down and the two of them were trotting on.

'They did it!' Kirstie gasped.

Lisa dared to open her eyes. 'They did?'

'Yeah, see!' Kirstie felt her jaw hang open, her eyes almost popping out of her head.

'They did!' Lisa gasped.

Brad brought Little Vixen round in an arc to face back down the slope. He came in a wide curve, kicking up loose earth and grit, which showered down the slope to where Lisa and Kirstie waited with Hollywood and Jethro.

'Yee-hah!' he cried, taking off his fancy white stetson and waving it in the air. 'Whaddya think? Ain't she the greatest little mare you ever saw?'

'Don't let him see we're impressed!' Lisa mumbled. 'C'mon, Kirstie; close your mouth, look like it was nothing.'

Kirstie nodded, agreeing that Brad's head was swollen enough already without any extra praise from them. So she swallowed hard. 'Yeah, Little Vixen did good,' she told him casually.

Disappointed, he sat back in the saddle. 'Only "good"?'

'Good enough,' Lisa echoed. 'But, hey Brad, you give Kirstie and me another day's practice and we can do that easy!'

'You can?' Brad's look expressed open disbelief. Like, no way could two amateurs like Kirstie and Lisa achieve the same jumping standard as the champion rider of the whole of Colorado.

So Lisa looked at Kirstie and Kirstie stared her right back in the eye.

'Sure!' they said together, as if with one voice.

They glanced up the slope at the Jaw-breaker log; high and wide, covered in scaly bark, its twisted roots reaching for the sky. 'We can do that. You just wait and see!'

3

Well, maybe Lisa was a little over-confident back there!
Kirstie told herself.

It was two days after Little Vixen and Brad had
conquered the Jaw-breaker, and still neither girl
felt quite ready to meet the challenge.

Then Lisa's mom had called and said she
needed Lisa back at the San Luis diner which she
ran almost single-handed.

'Just for twenty-four hours.' Bonnie had
explained the situation by phone. 'We have a
horse sale in town, which means dozens of

hungry traders who need to be fed, and the End of Trail Diner is where they'll head. I sure could do with the extra help, honey.'

'No problem,' Lisa had said, packing her bag and fixing a lift into town that evening with Matt. Before she'd left, she'd pinned Kirstie into a corner of the barn and put her on the spot.

'No sneaking extra practices on Jethro, you hear?'

Kirstie had come over all innocent. 'Me? Would I?'

'Sure you would. If I know you, Kirstie Scott, you'll be up on that training area jumping Jethro like crazy, while I'm stuck waiting tables at Mom's place!'

'So? Did we make any kind of rule about it?' Kirstie defended herself. 'I don't recall that being part of the deal. I mean, where's the harm in me taking Jethro out?'

'The harm is that it's not fair if you two get to train and me and Hollywood don't!' Lisa faced Kirstie, hands on hips, giving her a real hard time.

Kirstie hauled a bale of hay down from the stack, cut the twine and started to scatter it in the mangers where the brood mares were feeding. 'I take your point,' she'd conceded. 'But aren't we getting a little over-competitive here? This is a *fun* contest, remember!'

'Yeah, like the Fun Olympics!' Lisa had retorted. ' "Fun" as in "deadly serious" '

In the end, Kirstie had been forced to promise that if she snuck extra time with Jethro up on the training area, then she would allow Lisa and Hollywood exactly the same amount of time when Lisa returned to the ranch.

The hard-fought deal meant that she could get up early next morning, before any of the ranch guests were awake, and go out into Red Fox Meadow with a headcollar to fetch Jethro Junior back to the corral.

So early, in fact, that roosting jays were only just stirring in the trees by the creek, and the dawn sky was still tinged with pink. There was a white mist rising off the meadow, a quietness amongst the ramuda as the horses raised their slow heads at Kirstie's approach.

'Hey, Cadillac, hey, Crazy Horse,' she murmured gently, as the big creamy-white gelding and his inseparable companion approached through the mist. She went on through the meadow, patting

Yukon's soft nose and stopping to admire the way Rodeo Rocky had kept part of his wild mustang self intact by staying separate from the tame herd, keeping to the far fence and spending time gazing at and listening to the sounds of the distant mountains. There would always be part of Rocky that remained free, she knew.

Then at last she spotted Jethro's dark outline, picking him out from all the rest by the arch of his neck and the attentive way he stood. Always ready, always willing, he spotted her too and came quickly towards her, offering his head for her to fasten the collar and lead him off.

All was quiet and still when they got back to the corral. The tack-room was deserted as Kirstie went to lug Jethro's heavy saddle down from its rack. She slung the striped saddle blanket over his back, eased the saddle into place, then fastened the cinch. On the barn roof, two fat blue jays hopped and scrabbled along the metal ridge. From the slopes of Meltwater Trail, Kirstie heard two coyotes exchange their barking morning call.

'Easy, Jethro!' Kirstie breathed, as the dark bay horse pricked his ears at the wild sound. She stroked his smooth neck and touched his cheek to soothe him, waiting for him to settle before she hitched one foot into the stirrup and swung her leg over his back.

Then they were off, early and alone, riding beside the creek, noticing that less and less water ran through the valley as the summer heat dried up the mountain streams. The vivid pink flowers of the globe cacti stood out against the fading grass, while the spiky yuccas and yellow spears of the Indian tobacco plants spread as far as the eye could see.

This is heaven, Kirstie thought; half-awake and half-asleep, lulled by the silence and emptiness around her. Jethro walked easily, crossing the creek at the place where Bear Hunt Trail split off from the Five Mile Creek track. The smart horse didn't need to be told which direction they were heading, and he seemed eager to pass through the wooded slopes to reach the flat area of practice jumps where he and Kirstie could work out in peace.

So they arrived and jumped the makeshift course, rehearsing the finer points of balance needed to attempt the Jaw-breaker log. And it was a question of confidence too. Both Jethro and

Kirstie had to believe that they could clear that giant obstacle; hence the need for steady practice and concentration in the build-up towards it.

'Good boy!' Kirstie told Jethro over and over as he worked at the course. He felt solid and athletic, surefooted and fast.

They were going fabulously well. The little horse had found his rhythm and fairly flew over the jumps.

We can do anything! Kirstie thought. 'Me and Jethro are a winning team!'

But she spoke too soon.

They came to the highest fence on the practice course; a wide obstacle built up from logs and brushwood. Jethro had his mind set on clearing it. Kirstie was urging him on.

Then, *crack!* A sharp sound split the silence. The horse baulked at the very last second. Instead of rising through the air, his head went right down. He dug in his front feet just inches away from the fence, launching Kirstie forward over his shoulders, her feet flying from the stirrups, her hands losing contact with the reins.

Thump! Involuntary dismount. Kirstie was tangled up with brushwood. She had dirt in her mouth and a rip in her shirt. Her shoulder was hurting like hell.

'Jeez!' she moaned.

Did I break any bones? was her first thought. Her second was, *Is Jethro OK?*

So she got unsteadily to her feet, finding that the answer to her first question was luckily no. Spitting out the dirt, and gently easing her shoulder, she peered over the fence to find out where her horse had got to.

Jethro had careered fifty yards across the scrub, stirrups crashing against his flanks, loose reins trailing. Then he'd come to a puzzled stop. *Like, what happened? What the heck was that dreadful noise?*

Crack-crack-crack! The sound was repeated; sudden, sharp, far-off. Jethro reared on to his hind legs with a startled whinny.

Gunshots! Kirstie recognised the source of the shattering sound. Guys firing rifles over on Eagle's Peak, persecuting the poor deer.

Anger flared inside her. She swore as she brushed herself down and set off to fetch Jethro. 'How can they!' she said out loud. 'It's brutal, it's, it's . . .' Running out of words, Kirstie reached her horse and forced herself to calm down. Jethro was already upset enough, without her spreading her anger around.

So she carefully caught up the trailing reins and gathered him to her, reaching out to stroke him and lay her face against his cheek to still his quivering nerves. 'It's OK,' she soothed. 'That's gunfire, but's it's a long way off. Those guys won't harm you.'

Gradually, Jethro's fear subsided. His body stopped shaking and he no longer rolled his eyes or flattened his ears against his head. Soon he was normal Jethro; alive, alert, looking to Kirstie for what she wanted to do next. More jumps? More fence building?

'Let's go home,' she decided, mounting and turning him down Bear Hunt Trail. Her own heart was still beating fast with fury about what the hunters were doing. Killing made her sick and helpless. Hunting season: she hated it and the men in checkered jackets, with their rifles resting against their shoulders and murder in their eyes.

On Friday, Lisa came back up to Half-Moon Ranch.

'Show me another dirty dish and I'll throw it

right at you!' she sighed as she lay back against the warm earth and looked up through the trees at a perfect blue sky. Her day helping out at her mom's diner had been long and tiring, she said.

She and Kirstie had ridden out alone in the early evening of Friday to run a message for Sandy. The errand was to take a gift for Smiley's grandson up to Red Eagle Lodge.

'Smiley told me that little Zach had been asking him for a kid-sized stetson so he could look like his grandpa,' Sandy had explained. 'I happened to be in town earlier today, and I saw just the right hat in the general store. So I bought it on the spot. I didn't tell Smiley, so as not to spoil the surprise. Only, I find now I can't get it over to the lodge until early next week, unless you two girls can take it for me?'

As soon as they heard what it was, Kirstie and Lisa had been only too glad to run the errand. It gave them a chance to take a cool ride on Jethro and Hollywood, free from the friendly rivalry that had been building up to be the first to jump the Jaw-breaker.

'Why do people have to eat?' Lisa wondered idly, as she stared up at the sky.

The girls had broken their trip on the top of Bear Hunt Overlook, partly to rest their horses and partly to catch up on any gossip. Kirstie had already described to Lisa the incident with the hunters and their guns from the day before, and now Lisa was wondering about the notion that preparing, eating and cleaning up after food might be a pure waste of a person's valuable time.

'I mean, think of all the other stuff you could cram into a typical day if you didn't have to stop and eat.'

Kirstie only half agreed. 'Eating's OK,' she pointed out. 'The taste bit is real nice, for starters.'

'Hmmm.' Sounding doubtful, Lisa turned on to her stomach and began to pick at long stalks of dry grass.

'. . . Peanut butter sandwiches, tomato relish, waffles, blueberry pancakes with maple syrup . . .' Kirstie murmured.

Lisa begged her to stop. 'You're making me feel hungry!'

'Exactly!' Kirstie laughed, standing up ready to continue on their way. But as she moved, she caught sight of a fast moving creature blundering through the undergrowth some distance along the ridge from where they'd stopped to rest. 'Deer!' she warned, standing stock still and wondering what the scared animal would do when it saw them.

It was a doe, about five feet tall, sleek and slender. Her large, pricked ears gave her the name of mule deer; her dark eyes were big and staring. She was reddish-brown, merging into the pink granite of the ridge, and partly hidden by some aspen saplings whose roots clung hazardously to what seemed like a patch of bare, vertical rock. What was more, she seemed unaware of the two girls and their horses, her whole attention taken up by a source of danger coming from beyond the ridge.

Then a second, younger deer appeared, as scared and clumsy as the first. Its white throat stood out from the green branches, then it pushed clear and stood trembling beside the larger adult.

'What are they scared of?' Lisa whispered from her crouched position beside Kirstie.

Kirstie shrugged. 'Here come two more!'

Soon there were half a dozen on the ridge, ranging from the doe, through three yearlings to two small, sweet fawns who huddled in panic against the rock.

'Listen!' Kirstie crouched beside Lisa and pointed west in the direction of the setting sun. She thought she'd heard movement beyond a thick clump of ponderosa pines; maybe a twig snapping underfoot, maybe the roll of a loose pebble down the slope.

There it was again! The frightened deer heard it too, and started away in the opposite direction, only to find their narrow path blocked by a tall human figure with a gun.

'Hunters!' Kirstie gasped. She might have guessed it. Glancing over her shoulder, she saw two more men scrambling across the loose gravel surface of a shale slope to the north-west. They too grasped rifles in their hands and had them aimed in the direction of the fleeing deer.

'Hold it!' Lisa took in the situation and acted double fast. She stood straight up, legs planted wide, waving her arms over her head.

The interruption made all three men pause. It gave the deer the couple of seconds they needed to regroup and head off downhill.

As the hunters re-aimed and fired their guns, the deer jumped clear of jagged boulders, crashed through thorn bushes, then rapidly disappeared into the nearest stand of aspens.

Meanwhile, the badly aimed bullets ricocheted noisily but harmlessly from the trunks of the trees.

'What the . . . ?' The first man strode angrily along the Overlook. 'Stupid kids; you could get yourselves killed!'

Kirstie stood her ground. 'This isn't hunting territory,' she told him steadily. 'You're way out of order, mister!'

By this time, the other two gunmen had joined their leader. All were middle-aged men; probably city types whose idea of a macho long-weekend was to drive up from Denver to the mountains, buy a two-day licence and take a few shots at the defenceless wildlife.

One was thickset, with a dark moustache. The second was pale and wiry, wearing a yellow polo shirt and khaki trousers. The third wore a navy blue baseball cap low over his forehead and had thick forearms that were faintly tattooed with red and black snake and dragon designs.

'What d'you mean, this ain't hunting territory?' the man with the moustache growled back. 'We bought a ticket to shoot, end of story.'

'Not on Bear Hunt Overlook, you didn't.' Kirstie didn't feel scared of the rifles now that they were lowered and pointed safely at the ground. Instead, she experienced a sudden rise of the anger she'd felt about the hunters on the day before. 'You're on National Forest land. The licence only covers the private land beyond Red Eagle Lodge.'

'Stupid kid!' one of the other men muttered under his breath.

Lisa turned to give him the dead eye while Kirstie talked on.

'You taken a look at a map of the area lately?' Kirstie demanded. 'When you do, you'll see your licence to shoot ends over by Monument Rock, which is that tall, straight pillar on the skyline directly north of here.'

'Smart-ass!' the third hunter objected, taking a small oblong packet from his top pocket. He flipped the lid open, took out a cigarette and stuck it in his mouth. He fumbled for a match, struck it to light his smoke, then tossed it away with a careless flick of his thumb.

'Hey!' It was Lisa's turn to be really angry. She ran right across to the guy with the yellow shirt and scrunched down with the sole of her boot on the tinder-dry spot where he'd tossed his match. 'Can't you read the Fire Hazard notices around here?' she demanded. 'Or does that come along with not bothering to look at a map properly?'

'Jeez!' the man said, turning away in disgust. The smoke from his cigarette curled unpleasantly up Lisa's nostrils. 'That's all we need on our vacation: two jumped-up kids telling us what not to do!'

'It's important!' Lisa insisted. 'The land is bone dry at this time of year. If you don't take care over stuff like campfires and cigarette stubs, you could send the whole hillside up in flames!'

'Yeah, yeah!' The first of the men pushed past Kirstie and went to join his buddies. 'Let's get out of here,' he recommended. 'That bunch of deer is long gone. We need to find us some more.'

Frowning and scowling after them, Kirstie and Lisa watched the men shoulder their rifles and tramp off along the overlook.

'What are they like!' Lisa fumed. 'Great big, fat, ignorant slobs!'

'Yeah!' Kirstie sighed. The hunters were a

menace. It was the only part of life in the Meltwater Range that she really couldn't stomach. 'Listen,' she said, as she and Lisa went to untether Hollywood and Jethro from the trees down a narrow culvert where they'd found shade and water for them. 'I think we should mention those three guys to Smiley when we reach the lodge.'

Lisa nodded. 'Yeah, maybe he can get rid of them. And good riddance, I say!'

'Or maybe he can at least issue a warning about the fire hazard stuff.' Kirstie's hopes weren't so high. She was afraid that as the hunting and camping laws stood, they were stuck with the three men and a whole bunch more like them for at least the coming weekend.

'So we'll mention it,' Lisa insisted.

Kirstie checked the parcel in her saddle-bag – the present from her mom which she was planning to hand over to Zachary when they finally made it to Smiley's place. 'We'll mention it,' she agreed, riding on with her mind preoccupied, wondering what on earth it was that made supposedly sane, grown men want to put a bullet through the heart of something as beautiful, graceful, quick and harmless as a deer.

4

'Well, would ya look at that!' Smiley Gilpin stood back to admire his grandson while little Zach paraded proudly in his new white stetson.

'It fits just fine!' Lisa grinned.

Zach strutted up and down the porch outside Red Eagle Lodge. He wore the new hat at a stylish angle, hooking his thumbs into the belt loops of his jeans and striding across the boards with an ear-to-ear smile on his pointed face. 'Oh, wow!' he kept saying, swaggering his shoulders whenever he caught sight of his own reflection in the windows to Smiley's cabin.

'All you need now is the cowboy boots to go with it!' Kirstie pointed out.

'Yeah; brown ones with Cuban heels and lots of fancy stitching,' Lisa agreed.

Zach turned eagerly to Smiley. 'Hey, how about boots, Grandpa . . . !'

'Thanks a bunch, girls!' the good natured Forest Ranger muttered out of the corner of his mouth. He went to lift Zach and sit him on the wooden rail that ran along the length of the porch. 'Take it easy, one thing at a time,' he told him, removing the stetson and allowing Zach's spiky dark fringe to fall forward over his brow. 'First off, we have to make a good crease in the crown of this new hat. We can't let a real cowboy go around the place with a shop-made crease!'

Lisa and Kirstie watched the expert at work as Smiley patted the top of the stetson with the edge of one hand, denting the domed crown into exactly the shape he wanted.

'This here's a Montana crease,' he explained, 'with two little dents here that you make with the thumb and first finger, then a long one that you chop right down the middle. There!'

Satisfied with the reshaping, Smiley put the hat back on Zach's head and the little boy jumped down from the rail to run inside the house and look in a real mirror.

'You got time to share a jug of lemonade?' Smiley asked his visitors. 'If you have, just tie Hollywood and Jethro up on this rail and come along in.'

'You bet!' Lisa grabbed the chance to quench her thirst. She tethered Hollywood in the shade of a ponderosa pine and disappeared after Smiley and Zach, while Kirstie took it at a more leisurely pace, enjoying the cool of the evening breeze and the total quiet of the setting at Smiley's lodge.

She stayed outside for a few minutes to gaze beyond the forest trees, hoping to see a hawk or a falcon, or even a rare bald eagle soar across the pinkish-blue sky. But she had no luck. Instead, she caught the high pipping sounds of a couple of pika hiding their shy, mouse-like bodies in the nearby bushes, and further off the chirping whistle of a fat, yellow-bellied marmot.

'Kirstie, come and get your lemonade!' Lisa called from inside the lodge.

The clink of ice in glasses drew her into the

cabin, and she was quick to down the first drink on offer. As she gulped, Lisa did her usual thing – talk!

'Hey, Kirstie, I was telling Smiley about those guys with the guns; the ones who were way out of line over on Bear Hunt Overlook. And about the one who flicked his match into the brushwood.'

'I reckon I know who they are,' the ranger put in. He tried to ignore Zach, who was by this time busily making a lasso out of a length of twine and attempting to rope the arms of the beat-up red leather chair by the bedroom door. 'From Lisa's description, my guess is that it's Red Brooks and his two buddies, Garth Morgan and Vince McCoy. Red is the one with the heavy moustache, Garth is the pale, thin guy, and Vince McCoy has the tattoos up and down his arms.'

Lisa took up the explanations again. 'Smiley says those guys come over from Denver at least four or five weekends per year.'

'So they should know better than to shoot on National Forest land,' Kirstie pointed out. 'If they come that often, they know the rule book.'

Smiley shrugged. 'Red and co are city slickers

through and through. No way are they the real backwoodsmen they pretend to be when they're out here. That's all hokum. For them, it's kinda like Zach here playing cowboy.'

'Except with real guns!' Kirstie recalled the ear-splitting sound of the bullets as they cracked from the long barrels of the three men's rifles, and the noise as they ripped through leaves and ricocheted off the aspen trunks.

'Yeah well, you stay out of it,' Smiley recommended, noting the angry look on both girls' faces. 'Let me handle those guys.'

'What will you do?' Kirstie wanted to know.

'I'll pay their campsite a visit tomorrow, remind them that their licence to shoot doesn't include the area this side of Monument Rock, though they know that well enough already. I guess I'll also hand out a couple of extra Fire Hazard notices and ask them to take special care because right now the forest is just about as dry as it ever gets.'

'Bone dry,' Lisa muttered, still wearing a worried look.

It was Kirstie who thought it was time to change the subject. She kept one eye on Zach's antics with his home-made lasso while she dreamed up a weekend adventure that might include Smiley's grandson.

'Talking of campsites,' she began in a low voice that Zach wasn't meant to overhear just yet.

Lisa interrupted. 'Were we?'

'Yeah. Smiley's gonna visit Red Brooks' camp some time tomorrow . . .'

'I wish he could get rid of them totally!'

'Well, he can't, and there ain't a thing we can do,' Kirstie went on in a strong whisper, while Zach roped the doorhandle, tugged hard and shut the bedroom door with a loud bang. 'So anyways, what d'you say we three sleep out under the stars tomorrow night?'

Lisa cocked her head to one side as if she liked the sound of this. 'You mean, a camping trip for you, me and Zach?'

Kirstie nodded and turned to Smiley. 'How about it? Can you bear to part with him for one night?'

'Part with who? D'you mean me? What's goin' on?' Zach let go of his rope and leapfrogged a sofa to land in their midst. His brown eyes sparkled as he caught on to the idea that some exciting plan was being laid.

'Sorry!' Kirstie grimaced at Smiley. 'I didn't mean to put you on the spot!'

'That's OK, it's not down to you. This kid has ears as sharp as a mule deer's. He hears things you'd never believe.'

'So?' Zach insisted. 'Can I go?'

'Hold it. You don't even know where yet.' Smiley tried to quieten him in vain. So he nodded at Kirstie to go ahead. 'Let her explain.'

'How would you like to come riding out with us tomorrow in that great new cowboy hat of yours?' she asked. 'We got a real sweet mare called Yukon over at Half-Moon Ranch. She'd be a great horse for you, and she'd carry your tent across the back of her saddle, and when it came to nightfall, we'd find a place on the mountain to put up the tents. We'd sleep out under the stars.'

'Yeah!' Zach breathed, his eyes growing even bigger and shinier. 'Hey, Grandpa, you gotta let me go!'

Smiley listened, tilting his head this way and that. Maybe, maybe not. 'Zach's awful young,' he reminded them.

'I'm five!' the little boy said indignantly.

'We'd take real good care of him,' Lisa promised.

'And we'd have a two-way radio we could use if anything bad happened.' Kirstie wanted to let Smiley know that his grandson would be in safe hands. 'Don't worry; we won't let him out of our sight!'

'Hmm.' Still the old man hesitated. He had to consider all the angles. 'It's not that I think you wouldn't look after Zachary. It's just that I need to ask his mom and dad if it would be OK.'

'Sure,' Lisa nodded. She took the point.

No sooner said than Zach brought him the phone. 'So call them!'

Slow old Smiley ummed and aahed some more. 'What time is it in Europe?' he wondered. 'I guess it's morning over there. So that's OK.'

'Call them!' Zach pleaded, hopping impatiently up and down. 'Tell them I got a hat and I want to be a real cowboy!'

So that was what his soft-hearted grandpa did.

He called Paris, France. He spoke to his son and daughter-in-law. They said, 'Fine, no problem. It sounds like a slice of heaven to camp out on

Eagle's Peak, just like we did when we were kids. So go ahead, just do it.'

Kirstie and Lisa understood the outcome of the conversation and gave each other a happy high-five.

'Yesss!' Zach heard the answer from Smiley and punched the air. He sprang over the furniture, then turned a cartwheel out of the door on to the porch.

He didn't even notice that he'd startled Hollywood and Jethro into pulling at their lead-ropes and trying to break free. 'Yes,' he cried, leaping and tumbling out of the cabin on to the dry grass. 'Yes, yes, yes, yesss!'

'The kid's gonna be a handful,' Brad warned Kirstie. He stood in the corral watching the final preparations being made for the camping trip, noting that Zach was still in a hyper mood. 'You sure you and Lisa can handle him?'

'Sure,' Kirstie grinned. 'It's two or three hours ride out to Eagle's Peak; plenty of time for Zach to quieten down before we stop to make camp.'

'Plenty of time for him to get a sore butt if that's how he sits a trot!' Matt said in passing. He'd seen

Zachary give Yukon a good kick to set her moving around the corral. Then he'd watched as the young novice rider had jiggled up and down in the saddle. 'Can't you teach the kid how to post a trot instead?'

'Leave it to me!' Lisa offered, scooting over to the friendly brown-and-white paint and her breathless rider.

Meanwhile, Kirstie talked through the route on to the mountain with Brad and checked off her list of camping equipment with Sandy.

'You need to stay on the trail all the way to Bear Hunt Overlook,' Brad reminded her. 'Then you cut up to Monument Rock, but you don't keep on heading north. You turn to the west in the direction of Smiley's place. Zachary's grandpa is concerned for you to stay out of range of the deer hunters, like we all are. You gotta miss out the tract of private land where the hunters have a licence to shoot. That's real important, OK?'

Kirstie nodded. 'No problem,' she assured him, half her attention on Lisa and Zach. Her friend was miming how to post the trot for the little boy's benefit, sitting on an imaginary horse and talking, talking, talking . . .

'Did you pack three slickers?' Sandy wanted to know. '. . . Kirstie?'

'Hm? Oh, yeah, I sure did.'

'And enough food for supper tonight?'

'Yeah. We don't plan to build a fire and cook though. Both Lisa and me thought it wouldn't be good to risk a naked flame out there. So we came up with the idea of taking a thermos full of hot soup with us.'

'Good thinking.' Sandy seemed happy that Kirstie had planned things so carefully. 'How about packets of chips, cookies, apples . . . ?'

'Yeah, we got that stuff.' Kirstie reached out to pat the bulging saddle-bags slung across Jethro's back.

Brad looked at the pack and grinned. 'Looks like you could feed the entire US cavalry on that!'

Kirstie blushed. 'It's not all food. We got maps, flashlights, sleeping-rolls, tents . . .'

'Only kidding!' Brad laughed, stooping to check Jethro's cinch, then strolling over to do the same for Hollywood Princess.

'And you will take care,' Sandy persisted, laying her arm lightly along her daughter's shoulder.

'Mom, quit worrying!' Kirstie slipped free. She

unhitched Jethro's bridle from the saddle horn and carefully slid the cold metal bit into his mouth. Then she coiled the lead-rope and tied it against the side of the saddle. 'Me and Lisa have camped out a hundred times before!'

'Yeah, but not with a hyperactive five year old.' Sandy looked anxiously at Zach, who seemed to be picking up Lisa's riding tips quick as a flash. He was already smoothly posting, rising easily from the saddle when Yukon broke into a trot. 'You sure you got your radio?' she checked with Kirstie.

'Mom!'

'OK, OK . . . sorry!'

'Go on, get out of here before Mom has a coronary attack!' Matt recommended, passing by a second time. Saturday was his day for heading into town to take his girlfriend, Lachelle, to a movie. He was shaved and spruced up in casual sports clothes rather than the jeans and checked shirt he always wore on the ranch. Leaning into the tack-room, he called loudly for Charlie to hurry up and join him in the yard if he wanted a ride into San Luis.

'OK, we're all set!' Lisa decided that Zach had

had enough teaching for one day. In any case, Yukon was a steady, kid-broke horse who was bound to take good care of her novice rider. So Lisa shot back across the corral to fetch Hollywood, just as Charlie came rushing out of the tack-room.

'Oo-oops!' The young wrangler collided head-on with Lisa and put out both hands to stop her falling. They ended up face to face, with Charlie holding Lisa at arm's length.

'S-s-sorry!' Lisa gasped, her face colouring up like a traffic light. Embarrassed, she pulled herself free. Charlie stepped back to let her pass, scratching his head in puzzlement as she raced off.

Seeing this, Sandy raised her eyebrows and rolled her eyes at Kirstie. 'Do I see right . . . ?'

Kirstie grinned, then shrugged. 'I think Lisa has a big crush on someone . . . but according to her, no way!'

'That's what they all say.' In more relaxed mood, Sandy gave Kirstie a foot up into the saddle. 'So Zach,' she called. 'Bring Yukon over here and say goodbye to your grandpa. It's time to leave!'

Click-click; Zach moved the gentle mare slowly between the fence posts. He wore his new hat with its tall Montana crease, a blue checked shirt and a fringed brown leather jacket.

'My, you look great!' Sandy told him, catching hold of Yukon's reins and leading horse and rider out to Smiley's parked Jeep.

'Hey, Grandpa, do I look like a real cowboy?' Zach wanted to know.

Smiley clicked off the car radio he'd been using then leaned out of the cab window. 'Son, you look even better than John Wayne in all those old movies. I never saw a boy sit a saddle easier than you!'

Zach's beaming smile broadened still further. Perched in a tiny saddle on Yukon's broad brown-and-white back, he puffed out his chest then tried to look tough from under the broad brim of his hat. But the grin spoiled the effect, and they all burst out laughing.

'Get out of here!' Matt said a second time. He and Charlie were all set to drive off the ranch, but first they wanted to see the campers safely on their way.

So Lisa mounted Hollywood and the three

horses and riders gathered at the start of Five Mile Creek Trail. It was mid-morning; already hot and threatening to get hotter. There was no breeze, not a cloud in sight.

'You got plenty to drink?' Sandy asked, hovering by the corral gate.

'Mom!' Matt warned.

'Yeah, sorry,' she sighed, slipping a hand into Brad's. She nodded and gave them a small wave.

Clop-clop-clop; the small group set out at last, with Hollywood up front, naturally. The glamour girl tossed her flowing mane and stepped out with her long stride; a natural born leader. Then Kirstie let Yukon and Zach slide into place behind the Albino. She watched the rhythmical sway of the paint's slow step as they took to the trail by the trickling creek.

'Have a great adventure!' Smiley called out after him.

Zach turned and waved back.

Kirstie came last in line on lovely Jethro. Jethro Junior: alive from the tip of his ears to the last wisp of his black tail. Jethro the half-Irish, star jumping horse, who wouldn't be doing any jumping this trip at least.

Instead, it would be a steady, uneventful plod up Bear Hunt Trail, along the Overlook, up to Monument Rock. Today they would ignore the training jumps up on the plateau and pass straight by the side of the dreaded Jaw-breaker. Jethro might wonder why, and, knowing him and his boundless energy, he would probably want to work out as usual. But they would walk right on by with their tents and sleeping-rolls, heading for the hills.

And, as the sun went down, they would reach the mountain's shadowy, pine-clad slope, make camp and sleep under the stars.

5

Aspen Park was the area of pastureland where Kirstie's palomino, Lucky, had been sent to slowly recover from his hock sprain.

It was a wide plateau traversed by a stream which stood beyond Monument Rock on land Sandy Scott had hired from a big property owner who lived way to the north. High enough at 10,000 feet to stay reasonably cool throughout the hot summer, it was too cold and exposed to leave the horses up there much after late October each year.

The park wasn't a place Kirstie often visited because it involved getting a ride with someone who happened to be driving that way. Which was pretty infrequent. So she seized the chance on this parched weekend trek to make a short detour from the trail down into the shallow valley.

'We can stop to rest and I'll show you my very own horse,' Kirstie told Zach, who had quietened down in the hour and a half it had taken to ride Bear Hunt Trail. By this time, he'd sunk way down in the saddle and was letting Yukon make her own decisions about where she put her feet to cover the rough ground. *No more playing the real cowboy!* Kirstie smiled to herself at the slouching figure and the tired little face.

Zach perked up at the mention of a stop. 'Isn't Jethro your own horse?' he asked.

'Kind of. He's my horse while Lucky gets over an injury to his leg.' Even though Jethro couldn't possibly understand what she said, Kirstie still felt a pang of guilt at the betrayal. It was like listing friends in order of who you liked best. The one who came second would always feel hurt that he or she wasn't number one.

'Is Lucky better than Jethro?' Zach persisted.

'Not better. Just different. And I've known Lucky longer.'

'Huh.' Zach grunted and lapsed back into silence until they came down through the trees into Aspen Park. He spotted half a dozen Half-Moon Ranch horses grazing lazily in the valley, looking fat and content. 'Which one's Lucky?' he wanted to know.

Kirstie reined Jethro to a halt and studied the area. Her gaze separated out the white flecked coat of Snowflake, who was being rested because of a patch of photosensitivity on her pink muzzle. Then she identified dependable old Moose, who'd been brought up from Mineville, where it had proved too hot for him to stay and work at being a kind of tourist attraction for the Fraser brothers at their Buckaroos clothing store.

'There he is!' Lisa said suddenly, pointing to a horse which had just emerged from a stand of trees.

They all turned in the saddle to look more closely at the beautiful palomino with the almost white mane and tail. His coat shone in the midday sun like pure gold, his muscles rippled under the surface and his neck curved with the most grace and power it was possible to imagine.

For a moment, Kirstie felt a lump form in her throat. Jeez, she missed that horse!

'He's limping!' Zach pointed out from the far side of the pasture fence as Lucky strolled to greet them.

'A little bit,' Kirstie acknowledged. She knew from the vet, Glen Woodford, that these hock sprains took several weeks to heal.

'Let Nature do its work,' Glen had advised, once he'd injected an anti-inflammatory drug into the affected joint. 'Put Lucky out to pasture for the rest of the summer, and don't let him carry anyone on his back because that'll slow up the healing process.'

So here he was, idling the season away, growing fat and lazy.

'Hey, Lucky!' Kirstie murmured, dismounting from Jethro and climbing the high fence to speak with the palomino.

Lucky wandered up with a casual attitude; maybe he would deign to say hello, then again, maybe not.

'Would you look at that!' Lisa pointed out that Jethro's ears had gone back against his head and he'd begun to curl his lips and show his teeth. He swished his tail and stamped his foot to let everyone know he was there. 'Jethro's jealous!'

'Yeah, I know, he's in a mean mood.' Still, Kirstie needed to join up for a while with Lucky. She'd been lonely without him around the ranch, and she wanted to let him know this.

So she stayed a few minutes in the pasture, looping an arm round his neck and running her fingers through his pale mane.

Eventually Lucky seemed to forgive her for showing up out of the blue on some strange, dark bay horse. He began to take an interest by sniffing at her shirt and breathing over her neck and face. Then he let her rest her face against his cheek and stood while she picked grass seeds out of his forelock.

'Jethro's still looking kinda mean,' Lisa warned from her position in Hollywood's saddle.

'Yeah, I'm comin' now.' She gave Lucky one last stroke, then turned his head away in the direction of the thin trickle of clear water still running the length of the valley. 'Go drink,' she told him with the flick of her hand against his rump. 'Maybe we'll call by tomorrow, on our way home.'

And Lucky ambled off for water, limping slightly, happy to have renewed his acquaintance with Kirstie.

'Let's go!' Lisa urged. 'Before Jethro tries to jump this fence and pick a fight with Lucky!'

They travelled on in a line along a narrow trail which grew steeper and more rugged. There were more stretches of bare rock, fewer trees, and in the distance white patches of snow.

'When do we stop and make camp?' Zach asked wearily. His short legs dangled free of the heavy stirrups and he slumped over the saddle horn as Yukon plodded steadily on.

'Pretty soon.' Kirstie pointed out a point high on the hillside where their twisting trail intersected a wider Jeep road. 'There's a camp-site called Salt Lick Seven by the creek there. That's where we're headed.'

Satisfied, Zach nodded. But it was less than five minutes before he trotted out the same question as before. 'So when do we stop?'

'Soon,' Kirstie promised. She recalled all the long car journeys she'd made when she was Zach's age; her dad at the wheel, her mom in the passenger seat, Matt reading a book beside her in the back. 'Are we almost there?' she would ask over and over, until her dad would run out of patience and Sandy would twist around in her seat and say gently but firmly that Kirstie must stay quiet and learn to cowboy-up.

'C'mon, cowboy!' she said now to the small boy in the big stetson. 'This is an adventure, remember. How about, we three race to the Jeep road across this stretch of open country?'

The notion of a horseback race perked Zach up. He slipped his feet back into the stirrups and sat up straight. 'If Yukon and me reach the road first, we win?' he checked.

Lisa and Kirstie nodded. They formed a row with Hollywood and Jethro, Lisa gave the starter's orders, and they were off.

'Do we let him beat us?' Lisa whispered to Kirstie as the three horses left the trail and began to bushwhack up the slope.

'You bet!' Kirstie held Jethro back a little to allow Zach and Yukon to forge ahead. She grinned at the back view of the small kid bouncing around on the broad paint's back. His new hat had flown from his head and hung down around his shoulders, the fringes on his leather jacket flapped and danced as he half-posted, half-sat the ragged trot across the uneven ground.

'Log ahead!' Lisa yelled a warning, then grimaced as Yukon saw the obstacle and swerved to avoid it.

Zach gripped the saddle horn, jolted sideways, but stayed in place.

'Phew!' Lisa gulped and followed in the paint's footsteps.

But Kirstie decided to allow Jethro a small treat. She set him straight at the log and let him take a flying leap. He was over and thundering on after Hollywood and Yukon with a new spring in his stride.

'Give you something to jump and you're one happy horse!' Kirstie grinned, patting his neck and making sure not to overtake the others.

'I'm winning, I'm winning!' Zach cried as they drew near to the Jeep road. 'C'mon, Yukon, you can make it. Yee-hah!'

The paint flew over the final stretch, only stopping when she came to the dirt road.

'Yeah!' Zach cried, tumbling forward over her shoulders as she suddenly dug in her heels. Once more he managed to stay on board. 'Yee-hah! We won!'

Too wired up to notice what was going on around him, Zach hollered and ignored the beaten-up black Jeep that was climbing the hill. The vehicle approached fast, taking tight bends on two wheels and raising the yellow dust behind it. Even when the driver saw the three riders at the roadside, he failed to slow down, and simply went on churning up the cloud of dirt.

'Jeez, thanks a bunch!' Lisa coughed and spluttered as the grit got into her nose and mouth.

Kirstie had glimpsed three men in the Jeep as it passed them, then took a squealing left turn down the track leading to Salt Lick Seven campground. 'Guess who!' she muttered.

'Oh gee, not Red What's-his-name again!' Lisa guessed right. 'If those guys plan to use Salt Lick Seven, there's no way I want to share a campfire with them!'

Kirstie shrugged and said nothing, but privately she agreed. Telling Zach that it was clear for him to cross the road, they took a short-cut between two rocks and down a culvert that came out close to the campground.

The official site, set up by the Forest Rangers, was fenced off with rough poles and marked out into pitches, five of which were already occupied. Beyond the row of tents, there were big bins and notices warning campers to dispose of garbage with care, and at the far end of the ground there was a small shower block and an area for washing dishes.

'This is cool!' Zach's response showed that he for one was happy to spend the night here as planned.

'Yeah, hold it just a second.' Lisa frowned as Red Brooks' Jeep, which had taken the longer route off the road, pulled into the parking area.

The three men jumped out, slamming doors and talking loudly. They swaggered across to choose their pitch, bragging about the day's hunting and generally disturbing the peace.

'Did ya see that White-tailed buck up by Red Eagle Lodge?' Garth Morgan demanded. 'I had him in my sights, and I was this close to pulling the trigger, but the darned thing spooked at the last moment! Pow! I coulda nailed him real neat!'

Keeping to the far side of the campground, Kirstie glowered across at the men. She knew that hunters had no right to go after the rare White-tailed deer; that the species was protected by law.

And she knew that Garth and his buddies knew this too.

'OK, so what's the plan?' Vince McCoy demanded, throwing a long rifle case and a bulky rucksack down on to the ground. 'Do we set up camp here, grab something to eat, then get out there on to Eagle's Peak to see what deer we can track down?'

Red and Garth agreed that this sounded good.

'No way!' Lisa sighed and shook her head. 'I gotta get away from these guys!'

Little Zach groaned. 'I'm tired!'

Kirstie thought quickly. 'Listen, I know a really great place to camp. It's five minutes ride from here. We follow the creek upstream to that whale-shaped rock on the horizon, see?'

'I can't see no whale!' Zach moaned, scrunching his eyes and peering towards the sun.

'That big, smooth rock. It's not far. And we can make our own private camp with no one around. That's a whole lot more fun than staying here with a bunch of others.' Kirstie worked hard to convince him. 'That's real cowboy stuff; camping out in the middle of nowhere, with just the stars, and a creek running by your feet.'

'Hey, you kids!' A loud shout from Red Brooks interrupted them. 'I guess you're the ones who got the Forest Ranger on our backs!'

'Uh-oh!' Lisa realised what he meant. It seemed that Smiley had already paid the hunters a visit to warn them to take more care over the way they disposed of their spent matches. And it wouldn't have taken a genius to work out that it was Lisa and Kirstie who had informed against them.

The heavy-set man with the dark moustache marched towards them. 'Who d'you think you are, sticking your noses in? That Gilpin guy gave us a warning and threatened to withdraw our licence because of you!'

Kirstie and Lisa took deep breaths. They were afraid of Red Brooks' glowering look. Kirstie felt Jethro stiffen and grow wary, while Hollywood pranced sideways out of the man's line of vision.

'Now we can't shake you out of our hair,' Red went on. 'Every place we go, you show up. Well, you'd better watch out. Next time we meet up, you could just be in our range of fire!'

Kirstie felt a jolt of panic. They wouldn't dare . . . ! Her mouth went suddenly dry and she was forced to drop her gaze in the face of Red Brooks' scary threat.

It was Vince McCoy who stepped in to ease the situation. 'Back off, Red,' he advised, coming up alongside his buddy. 'They're only kids.'

'Yeah. If they belonged to me, they'd soon learn not to speak out of turn.' Still Red bullied. His small dark eyes shot hatred at them, and inside his temper boiled.

So McCoy tilted back the peak of his cap and turned to the riders. 'I guess you'd better beat it, the mood Red's in. You got some place else to pitch tent?'

Kirstie nodded. Staying at Salt Lick Seven overnight would ruin the whole trip, so now they had no choice but to head up to Whale Rock. Leaning sideways to catch hold of Yukon's rein, she and Jethro began to lead Zach back down the culvert.

'Yuck, do those guys suck!' Lisa muttered, ducking under a low branch. 'Just our luck that we keep running into them.'

'No, really. They did us a favour,' Kirstie insisted. 'It's gonna be so much more fun camping up by Whale Rock.'

'Is it still National Forest territory?' Lisa checked, remembering Sandy's instructions not to stray on to private land.

'Sure. So the no-hunting rule applies.' Kirstie gave Zach a smile of encouragement. 'What d'you say we pitch tent, then get out our sack-lunches?'

'Then can we swim in the creek?' Zach asked.

'Yeah, if there's enough water running through.' Kirstie thought it was a great idea, remembering a waterfall that tumbled down the far side of Whale Rock into a deep clear pool.

'Can the horses swim too?'

'Sure. We could ride them bareback into the water. How does that sound?'

'Cool.'

'Yeah, really!' Lisa cut in with a laugh. ' "Cool", as in "neat". And "cool", as in "cold water". We need something to help us through this heat.'

It made them yearn to reach their journey's end. And when they arrived, they were glad to find that there was enough snowmelt coming off the peak to have kept the creek flowing, even at the height of the dry summer. This meant they could water their horses and tether them in the shade of the humped rock. Then they could eat

sitting ankle-deep in the pool, perched on rocks with their legs dangling into the ice-cold water.

'We're trappers!' Zach exclaimed. 'We're fur traders pushing west into places where no guy ever went before!'

Kirstie laughed. 'We could build ourselves a log cabin . . .'

'Pan in the creek for gold nuggets . . .' Lisa suggested.

Kirstie took a deep breath, tilted back her head and felt the cool spray from the tumbling fall touch her cheeks. '. . . Or just chill out for the rest of the day,' she said.

6

Swimming, eating, drying in the sun on the baking surface of Whale Rock. That had been the challenging itinerary for the rest of that hot summer Saturday.

In the evening, they'd checked in by radio with Sandy and Smiley to tell them that all was well.

'Is that cowboy grandson of mine alive and kicking?' Smiley had asked. 'Or is he all tuckered out?'

'He's awake,' Kirstie had told him. 'He'd like to talk.'

She'd handed Zach the radio and he'd told Smiley about the small herd of mule deer who'd come to the pool at Whale Rock to drink. 'We never scared 'em, Grandpa. We just sat quiet on the rock and watched 'em. They was real pretty.'

Smiley had said that he was glad Zach was having such a great time and that he'd be sure to pass on the information to his mom and dad in Paris.

Then it had been time for a goodnight story, with Zach curled up inside his sleeping-bag and Lisa and Kirstie taking turns to tell him a tale they made up between them about a young buckaroo called Zachary who went punching cattle on the flat plains of eastern Colorado.

'And he worked cattle all day, and at night he went to sleep under the stars,' Lisa had explained. 'He rolled up his fringed leather jacket and used it for a pillow, and he hung his hat on the branch of a nearby tree.'

Zach had smiled and closed his eyes, drifted off into his dreams.

And today, Sunday, was fresh and new.

Kirstie woke early to the sound of the horses

grazing just outside her tent. She unzipped her sleeping-bag and peered out bleary-eyed, to be greeted close-up by Jethro poking his head in her face.

'Hey, how did you get loose from your lead-rope?' she murmured.

'Me. I did it,' a bright voice said. And there was Zach, already awake and wandering about the camp, taking it into his head to set the horses free so that they could breakfast on the best grass. Proudly he held up the three lengths of rope to show Kirstie what he'd done.

'Jeez, Zach, d'you want to walk all the way home?' she protested, waking Lisa so that they could both round up Jethro, Yukon and Hollywood.

They scrambled into their jeans and T-shirts then crawled quickly out on to the dewy grass.

But the horses were enjoying their freedom and smart Jethro soon saw what the girls were up to. He tossed his head at the sight of Kirstie taking a rope from Zach, then danced daintily around the edge of the pool on to a rocky ledge by the waterfall.

'Gotcha!' Kirstie followed the sassy bay horse

on to the dead-end ledge. She eased along, offering the rope and managing to clip one end of it to the rope halter that Jethro had worn overnight. 'There's no way out of this one, Junior, so why not come quietly?'

You must be joking! Jethro obviously still had other ideas. He took one look at the deep pool ten feet below the ledge, then judged the fifteen foot leap to the far side. Making up his mind that jumping clear of it would be a breeze, he sat back on his haunches and launched himself into the air.

Kirstie felt the tug of the rope between her hands. She let go before it burned, watched Jethro land on the far bank with the merest splash of his back heels.

'Whoa!' she cried, tipping forwards from the ledge and flinging out both arms to try and keep her balance. But her hands grasped at thin air and she was still toppling. Ten feet was a long way to fall; she saw the smooth surface of the water rush to meet her, then *smack!* she made icy contact.

Splash, gurgle, bubble! She sank like a stone, touched bottom, then pushed up towards the surface. When she surged clear, she found Zach and Lisa staring anxiously at the pool, with Hollywood, Jethro and Yukon forming part of the audience behind them.

'Grab them!' she yelled from her watery landing-place.

'We already did!' Lisa held up three ropes, each attached to one horse. 'No problem!'

'Jeez, why do I bother?' Huffily Kirstie swam to the edge of the pool. But by the time she reached it, she saw the funny side. 'You should try an early morning dip,' she recommended to Lisa. 'It beats a cold shower any day!'

'Yeah, yeah, well I'm happy to wait until the sun gets up before I take my swim,' Lisa countered, expertly tethering the horses to the trees. Then she went to rummage in the saddle-bags to bring out food for their breakfast, arranging small packs of cereal beside blue plastic bowls and spoons, then searching again in the bag for powdered milk.

Meanwhile, Kirstie climbed out of the water and went into the tent to change her dripping jeans and T-shirt. She came out towelling her long fair hair and looking round to discover what mischief Zach was currently making.

'What happened to our favourite five year old?' she asked Lisa casually when she saw that he was nowhere in sight.

Lisa looked up from spreading peanut butter on thick slices of bread. 'Did you check his tent?'

Kirstie put aside her towel and crouched to peer inside the lightweight blue and silver dome. Empty, except for a scrunched-up sleeping-bag and Zach's fringed jacket. 'Where was he when you last saw him?' she quizzed, growing slightly uneasy. After all, she'd promised Smiley that they wouldn't let his grandson out of their sight.

And this was tough territory for a little kid who didn't know his way around. There were sudden drops over narrow ledges, stands of ponderosa pines that towered overhead and blocked out the light. Not to mention bobcats and coyotes that would scare the heck out of Zach, even if they didn't actually plan to tear him limb from limb.

'The last I saw of him, he was climbing up on the top of Whale Rock. I told him breakfast was almost ready, so not to go far.' Lisa too showed she was anxious about Zach by forgetting about the bread and peanut butter and beginning to climb the granite hump to see if she could find him. 'Not here!' she reported back to Kirstie at ground level.

'So where did he go?' Kirstie double-checked the tent, then decided to spread the search further afield. 'Lisa, you stay here, OK? If Zach shows up, yell for me to come back. I'm gonna head down on foot towards Salt Lick Seven. I'll let you know if I see anything.'

Nodding from the top of Whale Rock, Lisa cupped her hands around her mouth and began to yell Zach's name. She got an echo from across the valley, but no reply from the kid himself.

'I'll kill him if he's fooling around!' Kirstie muttered to herself, setting off down the steep slope to the official campground. It would take her five to ten minutes to cover the ground and she would have to keep her eyes wide open. 'Zach, if you're playing a game of hide and seek, this isn't funny!' she called out at the top of her voice. Part of her still expected to have him jump out at her from behind a tree trunk or a boulder.

But she hurried on without picking up a single clue. And now it began to feel as if he'd simply vanished. One second he'd been there – a slight, impish figure in his blue shirt, white stetson and jeans – next thing he was gone as if the ground had swallowed him up.

What am I gonna tell Smiley? was the thought at the forefront of her mind as she hurried down the mountain. How did you break the news that you'd gone and lost the most precious thing in a person's life?

So by the time she reached Salt Lick, her heart was pounding fit to burst through her ribcage. She didn't even care that the only campers on the site who were awake and moving around were Red Brooks' two companions.

'We lost a little kid called Zach!' she told them breathlessly. 'Did he come by here?'

Garth Morgan, who was crouched over a small gas stove waiting for water in a tin kettle to boil, glanced up at her. 'We ain't seen no kid,' he said carelessly.

'Quit worrying,' was Vince McCoy's advice. 'Kids wander off. They come back. So what's the big deal?'

'But Zach doesn't know the territory.' Kirstie ran behind the tents, searching each bush and looking behind every boulder. 'He could've fallen and hurt himself. Anyways, he'll be scared to death if we don't find him soon.'

'Look, if we see him, we'll send him on up,' Morgan conceded. He fanned the small blue flames of the calor gas cooker to make them flare up higher and make the water boil faster. Then he got out a second stove and prepared to light it. 'We will, honest,' he insisted. 'But if you ask me, the kid's tying you girls up in knots, fooling around. If you hightail it back up to your camp, I bet my bottom dollar he'll be there.'

Taking a deep breath, Kirstie nodded. She noticed Red Brooks emerge from his tent, a towel over his shoulder, a bottle of shampoo in his hand. He headed for the log cabin which housed the showers, giving her his usual hostile look which sent Kirstie scooting back the way she'd come.

She climbed fast, hoping that McCoy had been right and that she would find Zach with a mouth full of peanut butter sandwich, sitting cross-legged by the pool.

But when she reached their camp, she saw the three horses waiting patiently by their trees, and this time no sign of either Lisa or Zach.

Kirstie's heart sank as she stared at the blue

bowls set out in a row. She yelled Lisa's name at the top of her voice, then rapidly scrambled up Whale Rock to gain a better view.

In fact, she could see a long way in every direction. And wherever she searched, she found that the landscape was silent and empty. Inching round on the spot, looking down over the tops of pine trees, into deep gulleys, along ridges, through stands of aspens and across rolling scrubland, she became more and more certain that something bad had happened.

'Lisa!' she cried. Why couldn't her friend have stayed on the spot until Kirstie got back? 'Zach!' Her voice carried down into Salt Lick Seven valley and was swallowed up. No sound came back up the mountain.

But there was something that caught her attention; not a noise or a strange movement, but a smell. It drifted into her nostrils and she registered its sharp, tingling presence. What was it? Breakfast cooking on Morgan's stove? Smoke? Yes, that was it; not a food smell, but the acrid scent of something burning!

Smoke! It caught in the back of Kirstie's throat.

Glancing across at the horses, she saw that they too were unsettled.

Then she remembered Garth Morgan's careless way with flames and matches and understood in an instant what had happened. He must have lit the second stove and tossed away the match, which had still been alight when it hit the ground. There had been bone-dry grass nearby. The flames had caught the wisps and spread. They had licked greedily at dry twigs. Fanned by a breeze, they'd grown within seconds to a serious blaze which even now McCoy and Morgan must be trying to put out.

Fire! The worst thing of all on a parched mountainside.

Kirstie felt the fear rise in her throat and almost choke her. So she set off once again towards the campground, scrambling and slipping down the hill, scratching her bare arms against thorn bushes in her haste to find out how bad things were.

And now the thought of Zach being lost fled from her mind. All she cared about were the flames and the drifting smoke that stung her eyes as she drew near.

She heard the crackle of fire, the burst of dry grass catching alight and flaring up, before she saw the flames.

Then she came round a tall boulder and looked down on a scene of confusion. Figures were running between tents, rescuing belongings before they headed towards their parked cars. They were shrouded in blue smoke, their arms over their heads to protect themselves from the heat, hunched forward as they ran.

Already an area covering ten square yards was ablaze and the wind was carrying it swiftly towards the log cabin at the far end of the camp-ground. Through waist-high flames Kirstie could see McCoy and Morgan fighting the blaze with blankets, trying to beat them down to the earth.

But as soon as they killed one patch, another broke out and devoured new bushes, so they had to start over, beating at the flames and crying out in panic for other campers to stay and help.

No one heeded their cry. Instead, they jumped as fast as they could into their cars and drove out, leaving the two men responsible for the blaze to fight a losing battle.

Kirstie herself stood transfixed about fifty yards above the scene of the fire. She could see that the camp's official fire-fighting equipment was out-of-reach of McCoy and Morgan, close to the half-hidden log cabin. And there was no resident campsite manager, she knew. Fear rooted her to the spot and clutched at her throat; something like this could take a real hold, spread up the mountain and destroy everything for miles around.

She knew these burn-outs; the one by Tigawon Springs had covered two whole square miles and had killed much of the wildlife that had moved too slowly to flee from its rampaging path. They'd had to send out planes laden with water tankers to quench it from the air. They'd moved ranchers from their homes and airlifted one family to safety as their home had burned around them.

And now that area was a blackened ruin with charred stumps pointing skywards where once there had been green trees and waving grasses. For years it would be an ugly scar on the beautiful mountains, and all because of something like this – a careless moment, a stupid act.

So she had to help. She couldn't just turn and run.

Instead, she fought her way through the clouds of smoke, grabbing a blanket that lay outside one of the abandoned tents as she passed. Soon she was beating at the flames alongside Morgan, feeling her skin begin to prickle with the heat, avoiding the sparks that flew into her face.

'Did you call for help?' she yelled at the hunter over the crackle of flames.

'No time!' he gasped back, beating desperately at a fresh flare-up. 'Maybe one of the guys in the cars . . .'

'Where's Mister Brooks?' Kirstie gasped. *Beat the flames down, kill them, drive them back into the dirt.*

'In there!' Morgan paused to point wildly in the direction of the cabin beyond the fire. The shower block was built tight up against a wall of rock and was by this time surrounded by flames.

The answer rocked Kirstie back a couple of steps. She took a break from beating down the flames. 'He's trapped!' she stammered.

Morgan nodded and fought on with even more desperation than before. 'We yelled at him when the fire first started, but we couldn't get to him. It spread too fast.'

'You're sure he's in there?' She watched the flames lick against the horizontal logs of the cabin, working their way higher and higher up the wall. Over the pitched roof, a pall of black smoke had begun to gather.

'He's in there,' Morgan echoed. 'Don't just stand there. We've got to get him out!'

7

Red Brooks might be a bully and an animal killer, but he didn't deserve to burn to death.

Kirstie knew this in an instant and clicked into action mode. This was a bad crisis; she needed to think fast. The best weapon to fight fire with was water. Natural water was in short supply in high summer, but the campground had its own, year-round piped supply. So where was the nearest faucet?

As Garth Morgan and Vince McCoy continued to beat a way through the flames towards the burning cabin, Kirstie ran to a stand-pipe. She needed a bucket or a bin, praying to discover something useful nearby that would help douse the flames. Better still, she found a coil of hose.

This was perfect. So, seizing it, she attached one end to the faucet, then dragged the length of the hose across the campground towards the fire.

Vince saw what she was planning and ran to turn on the water supply. Kirstie aimed the nozzle at the blazing cabin, then felt the hose jerk as the water surged through. She pointed the cold jet upwards, letting it spatter down on to the ground. There was a hiss and a belch of steam as the nearest flames died.

'More!' Morgan yelled, still beating the blaze with his heavy blanket. 'Keep goin'!'

Kirstie tugged at the snaking hose to extend its range. She felt water splash her hands and wrists and spray back into her scorched face. And still she kept aiming at the cabin, quenching flames with the jet and drawing steadily nearer to the burning shell.

'That's good!' Vince ran back to join them, standing directly in front of Kirstie to take the force of the jet against his body. He was soon drenched from head to toe and dragging his wet blanket over his head, ready to make a run forward through the smoke.

And Kirstie went on spraying as McCoy plunged into the dense black cloud. She watched his crouched, shrouded figure dart across the blackened earth, saw him wrench at the door to the shower block and tear it open.

'Please God it's not too late!' Morgan cried, rushing through hissing clouds of steam to join McCoy.

Kirstie aimed steadily, though smoke filled her lungs and the heat made her eyes feel red raw. Was it possible for anyone to survive inside the cabin? Or would it be a body that the two desperate men brought out from the hissing shell?

It seemed to be an age before McCoy and Morgan reappeared, but it could only have been a matter of seconds.

They emerged backwards, dragging a heavy weight.

Kirstie aimed the jet so that it doused their struggling figures. Through the spray she saw them haul Red Brooks through the door.

Dead or unconscious? It was impossible to tell. Still Kirstie directed the hose at the stubborn flames and held back the growing dread that the frantic rescue attempt had all been for nothing.

The two men backed towards her, dragging Brooks' limp form. He was heavy; they were coughing and trying to drag air into their choked lungs. At last they were clear of the smoke and they let their friend slump face-up on to the earth.

'Is he breathing?' McCoy dropped to his knees and stooped over Brooks' face, listening and feeling for any sign of life. 'I got a pulse!' he cried.

By this time Kirstie had dropped the hose and joined the men. 'Why didn't he get out when he heard what was happening?' she demanded.

Garth Morgan shook his head. He glanced at Kirstie with a scared, smoke-streaked face. 'We yelled for him to get out of there. I guess he didn't hear.'

'He wasn't feeling too good, I know that much.' McCoy had begun to work on a resuscitation technique that involved pinching Brooks' nose and breathing into his mouth. He seemed to know what he was doing, as if he had training. 'He said he was light-headed and a shower was what he needed to put him right. Maybe he passed out in there.'

'Then the smoke got to him.' Garth Morgan watched and waited anxiously. 'Vince is a paramedic,' he explained to Kirstie. 'So Red's in good hands.'

'What's happening? Is he going to be OK?' Kirstie asked.

'He inhaled a lot of smoke, but the inside walls of the shower block are tiled, which means that the flames were held back and Red didn't get any burn injuries.' Vince gave them his assessment. 'The point is, we gotta get his lungs working properly so they can pump enough oxygen into his blood.'

'I'd better call the hospital, get them to send out a helicopter with all the equipment,' Garth decided. He sprinted to the parking lot to use the two-way car radio.

Meanwhile, Vince's energetic resuscitation was paying off. Kirstie saw Red Brooks' chest heave and heard a spluttering cough. His eyelids flickered.

'That's better. C'mon, buddy, you can make it!' Vince urged. Then he asked Kirstie to help him turn Red on to his side and place him in the recovery position.

By the time they'd done this, Garth was back. 'Help's on its way,' he reported. 'A Fire Alert went up ten minutes back. They're sending firefighters and Forest Rangers. I asked for a doctor and they said he'll be here.'

'Red's coming round.' Vince gave Garth the latest news. 'I got more air into his lungs, but we have to hope that there's no serious damage to the lining of the airways.'

'That would be bad news?' Garth frowned.

'Yeah. If the tubes are inflamed, they narrow and starve the poor guy of oxygen big-time.'

Vince grimaced and looked around the wrecked campground. 'Where the heck's that medic?' he muttered.

'There!' Glancing up in the direction of Whale Rock, Kirstie saw a helicopter sweeping along the skyline. Its chugging roar grew louder as the pilot spotted the burned out campsite and brought the aircraft down the mountain towards them.

It landed in the parking area, its long blades rotating and stirring up ash from the recent fire. The sudden gust of wind blew new life into fading sparks, making the burned bushes glow red. New flames popped and crackled, made quick runs into untouched scrub and gobbled up the dry grass before fading and dying in the dirt.

Then people came running from the helicopter and Kirstie stood back to give them room. The paramedics strapped an oxygen mask around Brooks' face and eased him on to a stretcher. A woman doctor checked his pulse and breathing, examined the pupils of his eyes, decided on a rapid transfer to hospital.

'You did good work,' she assured Vince as the patient was stretchered off into the copter.

'Yeah, but it was all down to this young lady,' he replied, allowing himself a long sigh of relief now that help had arrived. 'If she hadn't fixed up the water hose, no way would we have got in there to bring him out.'

Exhausted, Kirstie gazed across at the smouldering cabin. It had been a close call, sure enough. As the doctor made arrangements for Vince and Garth to take a ride to the hospital in the copter, Kirstie looked anxiously at the continuing flare-ups in the scrub beside the shower block.

'Don't worry, the firefighters will be here any minute,' the doctor assured her. 'We were in radio contact. A couple of vehicles are driving up from a station by Five Mile Creek, and a ranger called Smiley Gilpin is heading his team down from Red Eagle Lodge.'

The mention of Smiley's name made Kirstie gasp. For the first time in fifteen minutes, she remembered Zach. 'I gotta go!' she told the doc, racing away from the scene of the fire up the rocky slope towards her own camp.

Though every muscle ached from the effort and tension of fighting the flames, still she had to force herself to climb the mountain so that she could locate Smiley's grandson before the ranger arrived.

'. . . Sandy to Kirstie. Are you receiving me? Over!'

Kirstie reached Whale Rock to the sound of her mom's anxious radio call. The voice spoke eerily into the silence of the empty campsite.

Still no Lisa, still no Zach. Where on earth had they been while the fire had blazed down below?

'. . . Sandy to Kirstie. Answer, please!'

Checking that Jethro, Hollywood and Yukon

were still securely tethered to their trees, Kirstie raced to pick up the phone. 'Mom, I'm here. It's me, Kirstie; I'm receiving you. Over!'

'Kirstie, thank the Lord!' Sandy's voice was choked with relief. 'I've been trying to make contact for what seems like hours! Over.'

'You heard about the fire at Salt Lick Seven? Over.'

'Sure. That was the reason I needed to speak with you. Are you OK? Over.'

'I'm fine, Mom . . .' Kirstie hesitated before she broke the news about Zach and Lisa.

'What's the situation with the fire? Over.' Sandy's crackly voice broke the silence.

'We got it under control. One guy got injured. They airlifted him to hospital. Over.'

'Fine. That's good. And you're not hurt in any way, Kirstie? Over.'

'No, really.' She turned to face the valley, looking down on the scene of devastation and scared to see small bursts of flame still flaring. 'Mom, where are you now? Over.'

'I'm in the ranch Jeep with Charlie and Brad. We're driving over. We should reach Salt Lick in about ten minutes. Over.'

'OK, listen. I'm up at Whale Rock with the three horses.' Kirstie chickened out of telling her mom the bad news. There would be time enough when they arrived. And by then it was possible that she would have tracked down the missing duo. So she grew brisk and practical over Hollywood, Jethro and Yukon. 'I plan to lead them over the ridge into the next valley because the smoke around here is spooking them real bad. The way the wind's blowing, I need to find a safe shelter for them to settle in. Over.'

'Good thinking, honey. And listen, you take care. We'll join you fast as we can. Over.' Sandy signed off for the last time and the radio wave cut out.

It left Kirstie with a dilemma. Should she carry out the plan she'd described to her mom and move the horses over the ridge? Or should she spend the next ten minutes searching for Lisa and Zach?

As it happened, she didn't have a choice. Hollywood saw to that.

The billowing smoke had got to her worse than the other two, and now, seeing Kirstie, the Albino horse started to rear and strain at her tether. It was her way of saying, *Get me out of here!* Kirstie knew that if she left her, Hollywood would soon injure herself by tugging too hard and kicking to be free.

So she ran across to the horses, careful to avoid Hollywood's flailing hooves.

'Easy, girl!' she said, reaching for the taut rope and waiting for Hollywood to stop struggling. 'I can't untie this darned thing if you fight me.'

Soon her voice calmed the frightened mare, who stopped rearing and stood waiting for Kirstie to loosen the knot. But her nostrils were still wide with fear and she showed the whites of her eyes.

Beside her, Yukon and Jethro communicated their impatience to be untied by skittering sideways and straining at their ropes.

'I know, I know,' Kirstie murmured, working quickly to free all three quivering horses. 'You hate this smoke. You're scared of fire and you want to get the heck out of here. Well, you and me both.'

Knowing that controlling three frightened horses would be difficult, she led them out carefully from under the trees and around the edge of the pool. Their hooves clipped the water and sank in the wet gravel until they reached the ledge leading to the waterfall.

Here Jethro tried to split away and tread along the ledge, but Kirstie pulled him back. 'There's no way out if we take that track,' she explained, picking a rocky slope to the right of Whale Rock and leading them on.

Hollywood whinnied as they climbed, sending a shrill warning to a bunch of mule deer that raced along the ridge. The agitated deer picked up the message not to descend into the fire-stricken valley and instead they veered away to the east, bounding on their long, thin legs, their white tails bobbing.

As Kirstie and the horses reached the top of the ridge, she paused to draw breath. Scanning the range of hills beyond, she saw that the rescue helicopter was already well on its way to San Luis. From this distance it looked like a weird metal dragonfly, its body glinting in the sun.

At least Red Brooks is getting the attention he needs, she thought, transferring her gaze to the dirt route which led to Red Eagle Lodge. So far there was no sign of Smiley and his Forest Rangers. But glancing in the other direction, back towards

Bear Hunt Overlook, Kirstie did see a vehicle on the trail and recognised the Half-Moon Ranch Jeep.

'Thank goodness!' she murmured, turning the horses towards Bear Hunt, anxious to share her worries about Zach before Smiley arrived.

But the Jeep was still some way off and Kirstie reckoned they couldn't possibly see her and the horses on the ridge. Besides she still had the problem of persuading Hollywood to behave.

'Easy!' she told her, using every ounce of willpower to sound calm and in control. Inside, the panic was building up again.

Hollywood sensed this and took it on board. If Kirstie was scared, then any self-respecting horse's instinct should be to flee. So the white mare began to struggle and rear again, thrusting Jethro off balance on the narrow ridge and barging sideways into Yukon. In the chaos of jostling, sliding bodies, Kirstie's arms were almost pulled from their sockets, her palms burned by the friction of the ropes slipping through her hands.

She cried out in pain and dropped the ropes, overbalancing backwards and crashing into a sharp rock behind. Winded, she doubled forward and, when she looked up, saw Hollywood and Yukon high-tailing it after the deer into the next valley.

Only Jethro had stayed put, waiting anxiously for Kirstie to recover from her fall.

'OK, good boy!' Gritting her teeth to cope with the ache in her ribs, Kirstie reached out to catch hold of Jethro's reins. 'You stand good and still while I climb in the saddle. OK, now we leave those two crazy horses to find their own way back to the ranch and we go ahead and meet Mom!'

Painfully she made it on to Jethro's back. By this time, the ranch Jeep had almost reached Salt Lick Seven and Kirstie had to double Jethro back down the mountain, this time avoiding the drifting smoke as best she could. The gutsy little horse overcame his own instinct to flee and obeyed her instructions, reaching the parking lot at the campground in time to meet Sandy, Brad and Charlie as they drew up in the Jeep.

'Jeez, what a wreck!' Charlie stepped out first and took in the burned out site. His boots crunched through burnt twigs, then he stood hands on hips, shaking his head.

Then action-man Brad jumped out and ran to seize the hose. Water still poured from the nozzle, so he aimed it at the random patches of flames that had kept hold in the bushes surrounding the camp.

Sandy was the one who saw that Kirstie was in pain as she sat uncomfortably on Jethro. She ran to her and helped her down. 'I thought you said you weren't hurt!'

'I'm OK, honest. But Mom, I gotta tell you something!' Kirstie spoke fast. She'd seen Smiley's Jeep approaching at speed along the Lodge trail. Before she had time to spill the beans, the Forest Rangers squealed into the parking lot and jumped out of the vehicle.

There were four uniformed men, including the heavy, slow-moving figure of Smiley himself, who headed straight for the spot where Jethro, Sandy and Kirstie stood.

Kirstie could see in an instant that the normally easy-going ranger was eaten up with anxiety. He came bare-headed, his face pale but sweating, his grey eyes haunted with fear.

She knew what he must be feeling: that it had been too big a risk to send his grandson off camping with her and Lisa. And now he was regretting giving in to the pressure, was convinced that he should have said no in case a disaster like this were to happen, in which case he would never – *could* never – ever forgive himself.

Then Smiley came up close to her and asked the dreaded question.

'Where's my boy?' he demanded, his eyes searching the empty hillside for the familiar little figure in his fringed jacket and white stetson. 'Did you take him some place safe, away from the fire? C'mon, Kirstie, take me to Zach so I can see for myself he's OK!'

8

Kirstie had never seen a grown man's face go to pieces so completely as Smiley's when she broke the news about Zach.

The ranger took off his hat, his mouth quivered, then a spasm of sheer panic contorted all his features.

'How d'you mean, he got lost?'

'He went missing before the fire started,' she explained. 'I set out looking for him down here. Lisa stayed up at Whale Rock. I was yelling Zach's name. I talked to a couple of guys down here, but no one had seen him. I was on my way up to meet Lisa, when I smelt smoke and turned around. The campground was already ablaze. I helped fight the fire, then I went back up for Lisa and Zach . . .' Kirstie stopped and shrugged her shoulders in a helpless gesture.

'You're telling me he got caught in the fire?' Smiley found it hard to grasp the facts. He'd begun to stride around the burned out camp, ignoring his fire-fighting team and looking wildly in every direction.

Kirstie ran after him, taking Jethro with her. 'No . . . I don't know. But I don't think Zach headed this way from Whale Rock. I guess he got lost going off in some other direction!' She wished with all her heart that she and Lisa had kept a better lookout for the little boy instead of letting him wander off. 'I'm sorry, Smiley. I really am!'

'Listen, there's no point going over and over this stuff until we find out exactly what happened.' Sandy intervened between Kirstie and the devastated Smiley. She drew them to one side as yet more firefighters arrived on the scene, this time the two teams from the station by Five Mile Creek.

Kirstie had to steady Jethro, who was freaked out by the sight of half a dozen guys in protective clothing, equipped with oxygen tanks and masks, piling out of the Jeeps. Together with the rangers, the men got ready to tackle what remained of the forest fire.

For a few minutes, they all broke off from worrying about Zach and Lisa to watch the teams at work. The men brought out more hoses, tree-cutting gear, axes and spades from their Jeeps. Then someone gave an order to clear the scrub around the burned area, creating a natural barrier to cut off the flames.

'The idea is, we cut down those saplings on the mountain!' The team leader pointed towards Whale Rock. 'The wind's blowing from the south. If the flames spread, that's the direction they'll take hold.'

So four men scrambled up the slope with saws and axes to clear a wide swathe of saplings and scrub. But Kirstie knew that, if the wind got up any stronger, this wouldn't be enough by itself. They would also have to douse the hillside with water, soaking the ground and hoping that stray sparks wouldn't fly across the denuded strip of land.

'Jeez, I can't stand here watching this!' Brad exclaimed. He'd worked hard to beat back small outbursts of fire around the cabin, and had spent some time clearing what was left of the campers' belongings so that they could be salvaged later. But now he wanted more decisive action. 'What d'you say I drive after Hollywood and Yukon?' he asked Sandy.

'Won't they head for home under their own steam?' she replied.

'Maybe. Maybe not. With all the confusion we got goin' around here, a couple of loose horses might just take it into their crazy heads to do something stupid.'

Charlie agreed. 'Let Brad find 'em and bring 'em in. That's one thing we know we can handle.'

So Sandy nodded and told Brad to keep in touch by radio. She watched him race to the Jeep, then turned back to Kirstie. 'How come Jethro didn't take off with Hollywood and Yukon?'

Kirstie shook her head. 'He just stuck with me. He's amazing.' Remembering how he'd stood his ground on the smoky ridge while Hollywood and Yukon had beat it down into the next valley, she put an arm round the bay horse's neck.

Jethro responded by coming up close and rubbing his head against her shoulder.

Meanwhile, the team leader from Five Mile Creek came to advise Smiley about the situation.

'We got a weather forecast through from the meteorological office in Denver and it doesn't look good,' he admitted. 'There's no chance of rain for starters.'

Dazed, Smiley nodded vaguely and turned the rim of his hat nervously between his two hands.

'And they say there's gonna be a wind up from the south.' The firefighter told it like it was. 'That's bad news for us.'

'Yeah, I see that.' Sandy had questions of her own. 'But you guys are doing good work here. Won't that be enough to contain the fire?'

'Not if the wind takes a hold. Part of our problem is that this hillside is laced with shallow underground tunnels. The fire's already gone under the surface; we got a lot of smouldering tree roots, and once the wind gets into the channels, it'll whip those roots into full-scale underground blazes that'll find their way to the surface and spread the fire where we least expect it.'

'Jeez!' To Kirstie this sounded horrific. Invisible fires creeping under the ground, exploding into the air from between cracks in the rocks and from the root networks under the trees.

'I hear you got a couple of people missing?' The firefighter checked out his information. 'So what I'm telling you is, you need to find them pretty damn quick.'

'You're saying this thing is gonna get worse before you finally beat it?' Sandy asked.

'For sure,' he admitted. 'We got planes coming in loaded with water tanks to spray the whole area, and we're doing what we can on the ground here . . .'

'. . . But?' Kirstie took a deep breath and spoke in a whisper.

'But we got the potential for a major disaster on our hands,' the man told them grimly. 'If you don't find your missing people within the next thirty minutes, we'll have no choice other than to evacuate you folks out of here.'

* * *

'We go back to the beginning!' Sandy insisted. She refused to panic, even though Smiley was in bits. 'Kirstie, think of the last thing you said to Lisa before you went down to Salt Lick looking for Zach.'

Sandy, Kirstie, Jethro, Charlie and Smiley were at that moment climbing up the hill to Whale Rock. They'd skirted wide of the firefighters' activities, avoiding the worst of the lingering smoke, and were now approaching the rock from the waterfall side.

Breathing hard, Kirstie tried to remember her exact final words to Lisa. 'Lisa told me that the last time she saw Zach, he was climbing to the very top of Whale Rock. She was making breakfast, but she dropped that and went up the rock herself. She said there was no sign of him up there.'

'OK, I got that.' Sandy took it all in. 'So you said for her to stay there while you went down to Salt Lick?'

Kirstie nodded, waiting for Jethro to pick his way across an area of loose gravel. The poor guy was doing his best not to let the situation get to him, but she could tell that the smoke and the noise of the tree-cutting equipment was bothering him badly.

'So that's where we start our search: on the top of Whale Rock,' Sandy decided. She said it twice in order to get through to Smiley, whose fear for his grandson was making him trip and stumble every step of the way.

'People can't just vanish!' Charlie said, to reassure himself as well as the others. 'Lisa and Zach gotta be somewhere around!'

As Kirstie led Jethro across the shale, she felt him take a quick sidestep and begin to slide. She hung on and slid with him, wondering what had upset his balance this time.

She soon knew the reason. As they came to a halt against a rock, she saw the surface of the gravel five yards away suddenly erupt. An animal was hastily escaping from its underground burrow, pushing its black snout into the daylight. Then a black-and-white striped face appeared, followed by broad shoulders then a pair of stocky front legs with sharp claws.

'Badger!' Kirstie breathed.

'In a big hurry,' Sandy commented.

The shaggy creature was out of his burrow in

seconds. Over two feet long, with a thick, grizzled grey coat, he ran clumsily across the shale.

'I guess it grew too hot for him down there,' Charlie said, recalling the firefighter's warning about the smouldering tree trunks and wind channels that might carry the fire by stealth until it burst out into the open once more.

The idea worried Kirstie more than she would admit. Maybe the badger incident was a coincidence, unconnected with the spreading fire. Then again, she knew these creatures never appeared during the day unless there was an emergency.

So she picked up speed with Jethro, with a sense that time might already be running out for their small, anxious search party.

They were almost at Whale Rock when what they had been dreading occurred.

Charlie was leading the way, with Smiley and Sandy close behind. Kirstie was bringing up the rear with Jethro.

'Hold it!' Smiley's sharp cry made them all stop. 'Did you hear that?'

Sandy shook her head. 'Hear what?'

They all listened to the whine of the tree-cutters, the whistle of the wind around their heads.

'That was a kid crying!' The old ranger spun round to face down the mountain.

'I don't think so, Smiley.' Gently Sandy tried to tell him that he was imagining it.

But before they had time to set him back on course, there was a roar behind Charlie and a red ball of flame shot out from a crevice in the nearby rock. It exploded into the smoky air, sending Charlie staggering, then licking up at the thorn bushes, setting them alight in a confusion of whooshing sparks and dancing yellow flame.

'God, that was Zach; he's down there behind that rock!' Smiley was still convinced that he'd heard the cry. He put up his arm to protect his face, then stumbled through the crackling bushes into a cloud of smoke.

'You OK, Charlie?' Sandy checked, while Kirstie fought once more to keep Jethro under control.

He nodded and picked himself up off the ground. 'The blast of air threw me clear.'

'So you carry on. I'll go after Smiley.' Without giving Kirstie and Charlie a chance to argue, Sandy plunged after the distraught ranger.

'Oh Jeez, nightmare!' Kirstie hated being separated. She felt they all needed to stick together. But she and Charlie had no choice other than to continue the search on Whale Rock.

They stumbled on, with Jethro even more spooked than before. But the horse seemed to trust Kirstie absolutely and overcome his natural instinct as they fought their way through the smoke which swept up the hill from below.

'What now?' Charlie demanded when they reached the waterfall. The small camp was as before; the bowls lay abandoned, Kirstie's towel was flung across a rock.

'We yell their names.' As yet, Kirstie wasn't able to think of anything more methodical.

So they called out for Zach and Lisa, aching for a reply.

Nothing. Not a sound that could be identified as human. Only the crackling undergrowth and the whistling wind.

Then, just as Kirstie felt at her most hopeless, Jethro took it into his head to make a move away from her side. He tugged at the reins, started to pull her around the edge of the pool towards the ledge leading to the waterfall.

For a moment, Kirstie imagined that the little bay horse was simply seeking refuge from the heat and the smoke in the cool shade of the overhanging rock. She was about to tell him, yet again, that there was no way through the other side, and that she didn't want them to be trapped there while this fire stayed so scary and unpredictable.

But Jethro seemed to have got it into his head to walk that ledge whether she wanted to or not, and she decided to give him his way.

She called over her shoulder to Charlie. 'Hey, maybe Jethro's on to something!'

He left off crawling into the tents, where he'd been searching for clues to the mystery vanishing act. 'Tell him this is no time to fool around!' he yelled back.

'I don't think he's fooling. My guess is he heard a sound back here!'

'I can't hear you! The water's drowning you out!'

Dropping Jethro's reins halfway along the ledge, she cupped her hands around her mouth. 'Follow us!' she hollered. 'C'mon, Charlie, make it fast!'

Kirstie didn't have time to say any more because Jethro had gone ahead and disappeared round a curve in the bend caused by a spur of jutting rock.

'Hey!' she protested. 'I thought you were too scared to leave my side! What got into you all of a sudden?' Scrambling after him, Kirstie's foot slipped on the wet rock and she had to cling to a tree root to keep her balance. Ten feet below, the water crashed into the deep foaming pool.

'What's going on?' Charlie had begun to race around the edge of the pool. He leaped on to the ledge, demanding an explanation.

'Search me,' Kirstie said, gasping for breath after her near-fall. She peered around the outcrop of rock, and saw with a shock that there was no sign of the stubborn little horse. 'Listen Charlie, I'm not sure what this is about. All I know is we have to follow Jethro!'

9

First there had been fire, now there was water to battle through. As Kirstie and Charlie rounded the bend on the ledge, they were faced with a wall of the stuff tumbling down the smooth hump of Whale Rock.

'See, it's a dead end!' Kirstie spoke her thoughts out loud. She'd always known that this ledge led nowhere.

But Charlie took a closer look. 'It can't be; not unless a wizard just waved his wand and magicked Jethro clean out of here!'

And Kirstie saw that this must be true; that somehow Jethro had worked his way round the waterfall and found a means of moving on beyond it. 'Charlie, you don't reckon this is the route Zach could've been exploring . . . ?'

The young wrangler frowned. 'It would take a pretty gutsy kid to tackle this ledge all alone. What d'you think?'

Kirstie worked it through. 'I reckon it's just the kind of thing Zach would do!' Cowboy Zach, fur-trapper Zach, Zach the brave explorer. She saw in a flash that the kid could easily have taken it into his head to do something crazy like this.

'It would explain why he didn't hear you and Lisa calling him,' Charlie pointed out, having to shout above the roar of the tumbling sheet of water. 'Noise from the fall would've blocked out your voices, however loud you yelled.'

Kirstie nodded eagerly as she studied the rock formation to the side of the fall. 'Maybe Lisa figured this out while I was fighting the fire down at Salt Lick. She worked her way off the top of the rock, down the side of the fall to this ledge. And then somehow she found a secret passage down here.'

Pointing to a scuff in the rock where a horse's iron shoe had recently trodden, Charlie edged his way wide of the waterfall. 'Jethro came this way, that's for sure.'

Hopes rising, Kirstie and Charlie pressed on. They found that the narrow ledge didn't stop at the fall, but curved back on itself, sloping down amongst some rough boulders, then entering an overhang.

'It's growing dark down here!' Kirstie breathed. Dark and musty, with straggly roots pushing down through the rock crevices, and damp leaves mouldering in corners.

'That won't bother Jethro none,' Charlie said. 'Like all horses, he can see just fine in the dark.'

'Yeah, but Zach and Lisa can't.' Kirstie thought of the point at which Zach's taste for adventure might have given out. It would most likely be about here, under this deep overhang, with the rock sloping steeply away, where creeping insects and crawling worms lurked in the dark.

And she imagined how much courage it must have taken for Lisa to carry on following him down what could well be a false trail. 'We need a clue,' she muttered. 'Something to show us we're on the right track.'

Caught between hope and doubt, they edged forward to find the overhang transforming into a natural split in the granite. The channel was wide and high enough for a fully grown person to make his way through; or for that matter, a half-Irish American quarter-horse.

'Jethro!' Kirstie found him blocking the way ahead. She spotted the glint of his dark eye, heard the chink of his bridle as he turned his head as if to say, *What kept you?*

Though she couldn't fully make out his dark shape in the gloom, she could sense the urgency in his stance. He seemed to know exactly the reason they were down here and to be once more overcoming a horse's deep fear – this time of narrow, confined spaces.

'OK, so you were right all along,' Kirstie admitted, reaching him and beginning to fumble in his saddle-bag for a flashlight. 'This is the route you wanted to take right from the start, but it takes us human guys longer to catch on.'

Jethro stamped his feet and shook his head. He blinked in the sudden shaft of light when

Kirstie flicked the switch of the torch.

'How long is this tunnel?' Charlie wanted to know. He glanced behind at the fading daylight, then along the black route ahead.

Kirstie shone the flashlight down the tunnel. 'I can't tell. It seems to bend back on itself and come out on the same side of the mountain we entered; like a U-shape.'

'That figures.' Sniffing the musty air, Charlie warned Kirstie that he reckoned he could smell smoke.

'No way!' she protested. Having come past the waterfall, Kirstie felt that fire was the last thing they had to worry about. Rather, her fear now was that there might be some deep, icy, underground pool which Zach or Lisa might have slipped into.

'Yeah, think about it.' Charlie was sure he was right. 'If this tunnel is a U-bend and it comes out overlooking Salt Lick Seven, then it stands to reason that the south wind can blow smoke through here.'

And when Kirstie stopped to inhale deeply, she knew that he'd figured it out right. Yes, she could smell smoke; she could even see the sinister, wispy curls in the yellow beam of her flashlight. 'There's a through-draught,' she agreed. 'That means there's a possibility of stuff catching light down here, like the firefighter guy told us.'

The thought struck her as total nightmare: being stuck underground and faced with another of those fireballs that had so nearly claimed Charlie up on the surface of the mountain. In this situation, there would be nowhere to leap or hide. The fire would explode on top of them, roll them up in its furnace and completely devour them.

Kirstie felt her hands begin to shake and saw the beam of the flashlight wobble against the rock walls. 'We gotta think straight,' she said. 'Say Zach came down this way and Lisa finally figured it out to follow him . . .'

'Hold it!' Charlie suddenly grabbed the light from her hand and pushed past Jethro to forge a way ahead. The thickening smoke made him cough as he stooped to pick a pale object off the floor of the tunnel.

'It's Zach's hat!' Kirstie exclaimed. She felt her heart jolt and momentarily stop.

'Yeah!' Charlie stood and stared at the bashed

and beaten object. 'Well now we're sure we're on the right track!'

Not knowing whether to be glad or terrified, Kirstie swallowed hard. She grew convinced that the smoke in the tunnel was thickening, that she could even see a spark or two whirling through the air towards them.

'Maybe we should turn around and go back?' Charlie suggested.

'No way! Not now we know Zach's down here some place!'

'Maybe he got out already.' There was a shake

in Charlie's voice, and little belief behind what he'd just said. 'No, OK, you're right. We press on!'

So Kirstie held Jethro on the tightest rein she could handle, urging him forward, asking him to trust her because she knew exactly what she was doing. 'It might look crazy,' she conceded. 'But Jethro, you want to save Zach and Lisa just as much as Charlie and me. And this is the only way, believe me.'

They followed the curve of the tunnel, expecting every second to see two small, huddled shapes of a little boy in a blue shirt and a red-haired girl. They would be too scared to go forward in the pitch dark, or maybe one of them would be slightly hurt. They would cry for help when they saw Kirstie's flashlight and heard the metallic click of Jethro's shoes against the rock. It would all end happily . . .

But no; the tunnel was empty except for the thickening smoke and the flying sparks. The wind seemed to suck the sparks down upon their hair and clothes, where they would glow for an instant then fade to specks of ash.

'We're coming to the exit,' Kirstie warned. Up

ahead, she saw an arch of daylight and more billowing smoke. And still the battered stetson was the only sign they'd found of Zach and Lisa.

'Maybe they made it through.' Charlie kept their hopes up as they inched forward. 'We're gonna get out of here and find them making their way down the mountain, asking why all the hassle?'

'We hope!' Kirstie muttered. She felt beads of sweat begin to stand out on her forehead, envisaged the whole hillside alight in spite of the firefighters' efforts.

With only ten yards to go, the heat of the smoke and sparks was intensifying. In the roof of the tunnel, threads of burning tree roots glowed red. Under their feet, burning leaves drifted along the uneven floor.

'If Zach and Lisa did make it through, let's hope they got well clear.' Kirstie's heart was in her mouth as she struggled to persuade Jethro forward to the exit. She felt him strain and pull back, as if his gritty courage was finally giving out.

And no wonder, because by now the heat was almost more than they could bear, and the scorching wind was blasting against their sweating faces. Kirstie ducked her head and pushed on. 'A few seconds more and we'll be out of here,' she promised Jethro, aware of Charlie coughing and choking in their wake.

The exit glowed orange through the grey smoke. There were definitely flames close to the opening; but maybe they were small enough for them to battle their way through. By now, going back was impossible because of the build-up of smoke in the U-bend, so the only way was forward.

'Get up in the saddle!' Charlie told Kirstie the best way for her and Jethro to make their exit. 'Jethro's too strong for you to force him on any further. But if you're up on his back, he'll respond better.'

Kirstie did as she was told, swinging up in the confined space of the tunnel. 'How about you?' she gasped at Charlie.

'I'm right behind you!' he promised, giving Jethro's rump a whack to help the scared horse on his way.

Startled, Jethro surged forward into the smoke-filled daylight. Screaming with terror, he broke out of the tunnel into what looked like a wall of flame, veered to the right and stumbled down a narrow culvert which the fire hadn't yet reached.

'Brave boy!' Kirstie gasped over and over.

Jethro went down on his knees, pitching her forward. Then he was up again, staggering away from the blaze into the gulley.

'Charlie!' Kirstie turned in the saddle to try and see whether he'd made it too.

'Yeah, I'm OK!' he called back. 'I took a left out of the tunnel. Where are you now?'

'I took a right!' Above the crackle and roar of the forest fire, Kirstie gave him her location. 'We're down a culvert!'

'Can you get out OK?' Charlie demanded. Then he broke into a new, startled cry. 'Hey, I can see Lisa! I think she got hurt . . . !'

'Charlie!' Kirstie begged for him not to go silent on her. She couldn't see beyond the flames, which by now blocked the end of the culvert through which she and Jethro had entered. 'What's happening?'

'Yeah, it's Lisa. She twisted her ankle, but it's not serious!'

'So where's Zach?' Kirstie yelled.

There was another silence which seemed to go

on forever while the whole world burned.

'Lisa says she last saw him down the culvert where you are. The kid was crazy with terror. He broke away from her and just ran.'

'OK, I got that!' Kirstie looked wildly around the narrow, tree-lined chasm. As yet she saw no sign of the runaway boy. But she was real close and there was a good chance she could find him.

'Kirstie!' Charlie's voice rose over the buffeting wind. 'Acording to Lisa, there's no other way out of that culvert!'

She searched on, wheeling Jethro around in the gulley. 'I hear you! But I can't see Zach yet!'

'We want you to ride out of there!' Charlie's voice rose in desperation. 'C'mon, Kirstie, do it now!'

She glanced back at the exit, at the flames moving swiftly across the gap, eating up bushes, igniting the trunks of trees and sending burning branches crashing down.

'Do it, Kirstie!'

'No!' No way could she leave a small, terrified kid alone in this gulley. 'Hold it!' she cried, in spite of Charlie's frantic pleas. 'Give me two minutes. I'm gonna bring Zach out of here if it's the last thing I do!'

10

Jethro twisted and writhed in terror. The inferno grew brighter, hotter, higher across the only exit to the culvert.

And still Kirstie pushed her horse on down the narrow gulch. She called out for Zach, searched desperately amongst the thorn bushes and aspen saplings, praying that he was still alive.

'C'mon, Jethro!' she breathed. By now, the little bay would have done anything to have her off his back. He kicked and bucked, reared and squealed. She sat tight, riding him rodeo-style, determined to stay in the saddle. For if she came off and crashed to the ground, if she cracked her head against a rock and fell unconscious, then that would be the end of things for her and the horse.

'Easy, boy! We'll soon be out of here!' Fighting him hard, she held him on a tight rein until at last he settled. He carried her forward up the gulley, every muscle twitching, his ears laid flat, hating ever moment.

'Zach!' Kirstie called. 'Where are you?'

Twenty yards behind, the forest fire roared.

'Please don't let the wind change direction!' she murmured. For the moment, it blew flames across the exit, but not down the narrow channel into the gulley. This gave her precious minutes to carry on with the search.

But from beyond the blaze, she could hear Lisa and Charlie screaming her name, begging her to turn around.

'Before it's too late!' Lisa pleaded, her voice faint and almost drowned out by the crackle of burning wood.

Kirstie glanced back. Tongues of vivid red fire licked the smoke-filled air. Trees had turned into tall spires of flame; branches crashed down across the exit. 'I'm OK!' she yelled. 'We'll pick up Zach then find a new way out!'

She hoped. She prayed.

'Zach!' she cried again. 'Answer me, please!'

'Over here!' The reply came at last.

For a moment, Kirstie thought she was doing the Smiley thing of imagining the faint voice. She hesitated, looked all around the dark gulley.

But Jethro's senses were more powerful. And he'd heard the sound. He pricked his ears and stood stock still, turned his head towards a twisted, overhanging ponderosa pine.

And there, at last, was Zach. He looked smaller than ever, huddled against the tree trunk, his knees hunched up to his chest, hands over his ears to block out the sound of the raging fire.

Immediately Kirstie flung herself from Jethro's back. She seized his reins and tugged him towards Zach, then let go of the horse and crouched beside the terrified boy.

'It's OK . . . you're gonna be just fine. Listen to me, Zach, we're gonna get you out of here!'

He looked at her with wide, scared eyes. He shook and trembled, and couldn't speak.

So she put her arms round him and held him

tight, telling him again that things would work out, at the same time realising that she must look scary herself, with her smoke-streaked face and soot-blackened hair. 'You see Jethro?' she told Zach. 'He's scared too, but he's not curling up into a little ball and giving in. Neither are we. We're gonna get up on that horse's back, and he'll help us find the best route out of here!'

Slowly Zach's wild gaze focused on the dark bay horse. He nodded as if he'd taken in what she'd just said.

'You ready to jump up in the saddle?'

Another nod. He let Kirstie help him on to his feet and clung tight to her shirt sleeve.

So she picked him up off the ground and carried him, hoisted him on to Jethro, telling the horse to stand still while she did it. 'Wait!' she instructed, turning back to the flames, cupping her mouth with both hands and yelling the latest news to her anxious friends.

'I found him!' she cried.

'Jeez, Kirstie, thank heavens!' Lisa's wailing voice carried over the blaze. 'Your mom's here, with Smiley.'

Kirstie took a deep breath. 'Zach's OK!'

she told them. 'He's just scared.'

'Honey!' This time it was Sandy's voice, full of undisguised fear for her daughter. 'Listen, I radioed the firefighting team and gave them your location. They're sending a plane directly overhead to douse the culvert.'

'How soon?' Kirstie yelled. *It'd better be fast!* she thought, watching the flames steadily eat their way down the gulley towards her, Jethro and Zach. Though the wind was still in their favour, it wouldn't be more than a few minutes before the fire reached them.

'As fast as they can!' Sandy promised. 'You hang on in there, OK!'

But Kirstie wasn't prepared to risk waiting for the as yet invisible plane. She had to take some action herself.

So she checked with Zach that he was safe in the saddle, told him to hang on tight to the leather horn, then vaulted on to Jethro's back. She found enough space to sit on his broad rump. Then, leaning forward, she was able to put both arms round little Zach and grab hold of the reins.

'Let's see what we find down the far end of

this culvert!' she whispered, giving Jethro's sides a kick.

'It just stops,' he whimpered. 'I already looked.'

Kirstie nodded and felt Jethro stumble forward with his double load. Luckily Zach was a lightweight and she herself didn't weigh more than a hundred and ten pounds. 'What blocks the way?' she asked, looking ahead to the narrowing gulch. The rocks rose almost sheer to either side, the pink granite surface glistening weirdly in the flickering light from the fire.

'A giant log!' Zach sobbed. 'I tried to climb it, but it was too big.'

'OK.' She urged Jethro forward between a stand of aspen trees, weaving their way to the end of the gulley. 'But maybe we can find a way around the log together.'

But when she saw the tree trunk that had been felled by the loggers and got jammed across the gap between the two rocks, her heart almost stopped.

'Giant' hardly described it. It was an ancient, mammoth pine tree, resting at a shallow angle a few inches from the ground. There was no room for them to wriggle underneath, but it raised the obstacle enough to make the mission of climbing it seem almost impossible. And there were no branches to act as hand and foot-holds; just the scaly circumference of the centuries-old trunk.

That's way bigger than the Jaw-breaker! was Kirstie's first reaction. She felt Jethro come to a halt and wait to be told what to do.

'You see!' Zach wailed, his voice breaking into sobs once more. Behind them, the fire burned on without let-up.

Kirstie had to ignore his cries and concentrate. OK, so Zach couldn't scale the obstacle, but maybe a star jumping horse like Jethro could. Yes, it was high. And yes, the run-up to the jump was slow and difficult. They would have to thread through the trees and approach the trunk at an awkward angle. Could Jethro do it with two riders on his back? Ought she to even risk it?

The answer to the last question came on a sudden gust of air. Kirstie gasped as she realised that the wind had shifted direction and was blustering down the culvert. She felt a blast of heat, saw the flames race ten yards towards them.

'Jethro, we gotta do this!' she decided. 'We got two or three minutes; no more!'

The horse seemed to understand what she planned. He took a good look at the fallen tree, then allowed himself to be wheeled around and headed back through the aspens to a small clearing. Kirstie turned him again, held him back while they worked out the best route through the trees.

'I'm scared!' Zach cried, gripping the saddle horn until his knuckles were white.

'Hold on tight!' she told him firmly. 'Close your eyes if you don't want to look!'

Another roar of flames and still more heat on their backs told her it was time to do it.

'OK, Jethro, this is the most important jump you ever made in your entire life!' she told him through gritted teeth.

The bay horse braced himself and looked straight ahead.

'If you mess this up, we're dead!' she whispered.

He gathered himself and focused on the obstacle.

Kirstie sensed his determination and courage. She put her faith in Jethro and kicked him forward.

With the smoke billowing behind and sparks flying, he took off through the aspens. He wove

to left and right. Kirstie and Zach ducked low branches, brushed past spiky limbs, held on for dear life.

Jethro thundered towards the tree trunk without flinching. As they drew near, it seemed to rise even higher. It was dark, solid, rough – insurmountable.

'Oh, Jeez!' Kirstie breathed.

The little horse took the trunk at breakneck speed. He raised his forelegs and pushed off with the back ones. They were soaring through the air. Up, and up, like they were flying. Then over and down.

They landed with a thud, the breath almost knocked out of them, dazed by the hugeness of what Jethro had done.

That was Sunday. Today was Wednesday, and, except for the burn-out at Salt Lick Seven, it was as if the crisis had never happened.

Kirstie was riding out with Lisa on Jethro and Hollywood, thankful for a break in the unbroken blue skies of August. This morning there were clouds over Eagle's Peak and the forecast of certain rain before the evening was out.

They were heading for the Jaw-breaker and the ultimate jumping contest between their two horses.

'So anyways, when you, Zach and Jethro loped around the side of that culvert, we couldn't believe our eyes!' Lisa recalled the scene. 'I'm thinking, this is an illusion, it can't be real!'

'How d'you think I felt?' Kirstie had been the first to admit that Jethro's feat had been truly amazing. She remembered how her mom had run towards them, arms wide; how Smiley had broken down and wept.

Then Jethro had pulled up amongst the clouds of smoke, coughing and snorting, playing up again now that he'd completed his mission of jumping the trunk.

Sandy had run forward and lifted Zach out of the saddle. Smiley had taken his grandson from her and hugged him to his chest. For a full five minutes, neither the sobbing boy nor the distraught man had been able to utter a word.

Not until the plane had droned into view over Whale Rock did anyone really believe what had taken place. Then the shower of cold water from the tanks on the plane had brought them round. They'd turned up their faces, and their tears had mingled with the artificial rain. Charlie had hugged Lisa, Lisa had hugged Kirstie, Sandy had put her arms round everyone in sight.

And the fire-fighting planes, combined with the teams on the ground, had brought the forest fire under control at last. By Sunday evening, the surface flames had died to black ash. Working on through the night and into Monday, the teams from Five Mile Creek had pumped water into the underground crevices and tunnels, and by the end of the second day, the smouldering roots had been extinguished.

'Good job!' The head of the teams had congratulated his men in the yard at Half-Moon Ranch. They'd agreed to rendezvous there when the task was done. Then the head guy had made a special point of complimenting Kirstie and Jethro.

'You did real good,' he'd told them. 'I don't know another horse who would've taken on going through that smoke-filled tunnel looking for the kid. Not to mention clearing that trunk out of the culvert.'

Kirstie had blushed and grinned. 'Yeah, Jethro's a star.'

And they'd got news from the hospital on Monday that Red Brooks was recovering. They'd diagnosed a low blood pressure problem that had caused him to feel dizzy and pass out in the shower block, then they'd confirmed that the smoke inhalation hadn't permanently damaged his lungs. He would be home in Denver in a couple of days' time.

'And back up on Eagle's Peak, shooting the deer, soon after,' Lisa had muttered darkly.

'Yeah!' Kirstie had sighed, acknowledging that there were some problems in the world that you just couldn't solve right away.

Then there'd been Tuesday for everyone to settle down into routine. Zach had visited the ranch with his grandpa to show them the new pair of cowboy boots Smiley had bought for him in San Luis that morning. He'd strutted around like Clint Eastwood, giving Kirstie and Lisa mean, moody looks.

And Smiley and Zach had promised to drive up to the Jaw-breaker today, to join Sandy, Brad and Charlie to make up the audience for the ultimate jumping contest.

'Feeling jittery?' Kirstie asked Lisa as they

approached the training ground.

'A little.' Lisa took Hollywood over a couple of practice jumps. 'But I reckon we can do it.'

Kirstie saw the small bunch of people over by the Jaw-breaker. She gave them a wave and told them that they were almost ready. 'Jethro's gonna walk this baby!' she promised them, as she followed Lisa down the slope to the starting-point for the test-jump.

It was already decided that Lisa and Hollywood Princess would be the first to attempt the jump.

'Way to go, Lisa!' Charlie took off his hat and waved it in the air as horse and rider set off.

'Way to go!' Zach echoed, sitting astride his grandpa's broad shoulders.

Kirstie watched her friend thunder up the slope over the soft earth. Hollywood judged it just right; a good speed, good control, perfect balance. She took off and soared through the air, landed gracefully and loped on.

'Yee-hah!' Charlie cried.

Everyone clapped and cheered.

'OK, Jethro!' Kirstie muttered. 'We can do this, no problem!' She pointed him at the Jaw-breaker, urged him forward up the hill.

She saw her mom's face, relaxed and smiling. She saw Brad's arm round Sandy's shoulder. She heard Zach cry out, 'Way to go!'

Jethro reached the log all wrong. His stride was uneven, his balance thrown. 'C'mon, boy!' Kirstie cried.

But instead of taking off, the little bay horse dug in his heels. He came to the sharpest halt anyone ever saw.

And Kirstie shot over the Jaw-breaker, but she did it minus her horse.

She landed on the far side in the dust and dirt.

Jethro veered off away from the log and downhill. He was heading at a gallop straight for home.

'Involuntary dismount!' Charlie cried. 'That makes Lisa and Hollywood the out and out winner!'

And pride comes before a fall, Kirstie told herself ruefully as she picked herself up and dusted herself down. She spat earth from her mouth and picked pine needles from her hair.

'That's the big problem about riding horses,' Brad laughed. 'No way can a guy make out what fool thing the darned critter is gonna do next!'